The Baldasseri Royals

Destined to rule...*and* live happily-ever-after?

Welcome to San Vantino...home to siblings Prince Rini, Prince Vincenzo and Princess Bella Baldasseri. The family may appear to live a charmed life—they're royalty, after all!—but that doesn't mean that every day is plain sailing.

Now they must face their greatest challenge. Can they devote themselves to their kingdom *and* let themselves find true love? Well...we're about to find out!

Step inside the palace with...

Rini and Luna's story
Reclaiming the Prince's Heart

Vincenzo and Francesca's story
Falling for the Baldasseri Prince
Available now!

Bella and Luca's story
Coming soon!

Dear Reader,

How many times in your life have you thought you understood what was happening, and then you learned a truth that changed your entire perception?

In my book *Falling for the Baldasseri Prince*, such a situation exists. A shocking revelation has affected two royal houses and thrown all their lives into chaos. It's one thing to believe in a silver lining, but quite another for a miracle to happen. I hope you'll be thrilled by this miracle that affects so many lives...

Enjoy!

Rebecca Winters

Falling for the Baldasseri Prince

Rebecca Winters

HARLEQUIN®

Romance™

Recycling programs
for this product may
not exist in your area.

ISBN-13: 978-1-335-40695-8

Falling for the Baldasseri Prince

Copyright © 2022 by Rebecca Winters

This edition published by arrangement with Harlequin Books S.A.

For questions and comments about the quality of this book,
please contact us at CustomerService@Harlequin.com.

Harlequin Enterprises ULC
22 Adelaide St. West, 41st Floor
Toronto, Ontario M5H 4E3, Canada
www.Harlequin.com

Printed in U.S.A.

Rebecca Winters lives in Salt Lake City, Utah. With canyons and high alpine meadows full of wildflowers, she never runs out of places to explore. They, plus her favorite vacation spots in Europe, often end up as backgrounds for her romance novels—because writing is her passion, along with her family and church. Rebecca loves to hear from readers. If you wish to email her, please visit her website at rebeccawinters.net.

Books by Rebecca Winters

Harlequin Romance

The Baldasseri Royals

Reclaiming the Prince's Heart

Secrets of a Billionaire

The Greek's Secret Heir
Unmasking the Secret Prince

Escape to Provence

Falling for Her French Tycoon
Falling for His Unlikely Cinderella

The Princess Brides

The Princess's New Year Wedding
The Prince's Forbidden Bride
How to Propose to a Princess

Visit the Author Profile page
at Harlequin.com for more titles.

To my wonderful parents, who gave me a beautiful life and helped me believe miracles happen more often than we know. Their faith, goodness and love have made this experience on earth magical for me. I'll never be able to thank them enough.

Praise for
Rebecca Winters

"This is the first book that I have read by this author but definitely not the last as it is an amazing story. I definitely recommend this book as it is so well written and definitely worth reading."

—*Goodreads* on *How to Propose to a Princess*

CHAPTER ONE

Bern, Switzerland, early July

"WELL, SIS. HAVE you made a decision yet?"

Francesca Visconti pored over the information on the computer in her bedroom. She'd been living at home with her parents since her graduation last week from the University of Milan in Italy to become a veterinarian. "After careful consideration, there's an opening for a vet in France and one in Germany. Both sound promising."

"But?"

"There's another opening in Switzerland. Every professor of mine has talked about the head of that clinic. Dr. Daniel Zoller, the owner, is legendary. To get a position with him would be a dream come true. It's located near a biosphere reserve in the most breathtaking country on earth. I've been looking at the videos. The place is fabulous!"

"Why do I get the feeling there's a problem?"

"There are two actually."

"Start with the first one."

"One of the qualifications is that I would have to speak Romansh."

"Why?"

She smiled at Rolf who stood next to her. "Because the clinic is located in eastern Switzerland where Romansh is only spoken by a small percentage of the population."

"It must be tiny. You speak four other languages. That ought to be enough."

"But not the one that will get me this coveted position."

"How many qualified people applying will know that language?"

She blinked. "I have no idea."

"If I were you, I'd apply for it anyway because you've got more outstanding credentials than anyone I know."

Francesca looked up at him. "My fan club. What would I do without you?"

"If I recall, you were the one who encouraged me to go to graduate school in Paris.

My French was horrible, but you helped me. Now I'm close to graduating and it's all because of you."

"I didn't do that much, but thank you."

"You're welcome. Now tell me the other problem."

"It's beyond serious."

He sat on the corner of her desk. "I'm listening."

"You and I grew up hearing about the battle between the House of Baldasseri in Switzerland and the House of Visconti in Italy. Three hundred years of fighting went on over the massive timber rights in eastern Switzerland they both claimed."

"Yup. And when the Baldasseri family prevailed, the Visconti family never got over it. The feud carried down over the years. Papa said life in their household was a living nightmare."

She nodded. "He's always said his brother Stefano was the personification of their dictatorial father and grandfather. Once they were dead, he was determined to claim those timber rights for their family."

"He's out of control. Dad said that when Stefano became head of the family, he was such a tyrant, he wouldn't even allow Papa to marry Mamma because she was a commoner. Dad married her anyway and Stefano turned it into a scandal that fed the media news and drove our father away."

"It's a horrible story," Francesca murmured. "Papa gave up his title for her and left Italy."

"Thank heaven."

"Agreed, but guess what? It looks like Stefano, in all his fury, has found a way at last to get his hands on those timber holdings."

"How?"

"Did you watch the news last night?"

"No. I was out with Gina."

"Well, at the end of the month, our estranged cousin Princess Valentina Visconti, our uncle Stefano's only child, is marrying Prince Baldasseri of Scuol."

"You're kidding! How did he manage that?"

"Who knows, and now I have a real problem. Take a look at this map of eastern Switzerland." She enlarged it for him. "The veterinarian clinic where I'd give anything to work is here in Zernez. The Baldasseri Palace is there in Scuol. The two towns are a twenty-minute drive apart.

"Do I dare apply for the position of veterinarian when my last name is Visconti, and Valentina Visconti is my cousin? What if word gets around that a Visconti is working at the clinic? I wouldn't want to do anything that would create more trouble for Papa here in Switzerland. Not after Stefano drove him out of Italy with his cruelty."

Her brother stood up for a better look. It took a second before he said, "Why don't you make up a new name?"

"Rolf…"

"Impress the clinic owner by introducing yourself with a Romansh surname. Look up a bunch and let's pick your favorite." He grinned.

Her brother could be a rascal, but he had a brilliant mind. Following up on his suggestion, she produced a list of Romansh names. "Do you like Andrin?"

He shook his head.

"Here's Gori."

"No way." They kept studying them until Rolf said, "How about Linard? It's German Swiss for Leonhard and Lienhard."

"Linard…" she said the name several times. "I like it."

"That's a keeper." They both chuckled.

"Of course, I'd have to tell Dr. Zoller everything first. And if a miracle happened and I got the job, I would have to find a place to live in Zernez."

"Let's look at some rentals right now."

She researched available housing. "Oh, Rolf. Look at all these darling Swiss chalets. It's like wonderland."

He nodded. "The prices are reasonable too."

"I really like this apartment. It's adorable with all those window boxes full of flowers."

"Better investigate the inside first."

She studied the information on the home page. "It says two bedrooms." To her delight the interior looked exactly like what she wanted. "It'll be available in a week. If I lived there, you and Gina could come and stay with me sometimes."

"You can count on it."

She turned to him. "I'm getting ahead of myself, Rolf."

"Have you filled out all the paperwork and application for that clinic?"

"Yes, but I've been afraid to send it."

"Don't forget our father's favorite slogan.

'What we fear doing most is usually what we most need to do.'"

She jumped up and gave him a hug. "I'm so glad you're home this weekend. I'm going to send it in right now and see what happens."

Three days later Francesca received a response asking her to come for the initial interview to discuss the scope and expectations of the position. "At least I wasn't denied an interview right off," she told Rolf on the phone. He'd gone back to Paris.

"What name did you use?"

"Visconti. I had to since all my work and transcripts have my name on them."

"I get it. Just remember. This is only the beginning, Francesca. When is the interview?"

"Tomorrow at one o'clock. I'm going to take the train and rent a car after I get there."

"Sounds exciting. Call me tomorrow after you've met the paragon."

"You know I will."

At four in the afternoon of the next day, Francesca felt like she was floating on a cloud. She got in the rental car, deciding to drive back to Bern. She needed to process all that had happened. Hunger drove her to stop at a drive-through for a meal. While she ate, she phoned her brother.

"Rolf Visconti?"

"Francesca?" he cried.

"This is Dr. Linard who has promised to learn Romansh as fast as possible."

"I knew it! You got the position!"

"It's all so wonderful, *he's* so wonderful, I don't know where to begin. When I explained about Papa and the Visconti family, Dr. Zoller said he'd arrange for a government regulator to give me a waiver to use a different name at the clinic. Can you believe it?"

"I can, and I think you're too excited to talk coherently."

"I am." Tears poured down her cheeks. "I'll never be able to thank you enough for pushing me into sending in my papers. The clinic is incredible, and my position includes occasionally working with a biologist at the nearby bioreserve. This is a once in a lifetime opportunity for me and I'm so grateful."

"No one has studied harder or deserves it more."

"Thanks, dear brother. While I'm still here, I'm going to drive to that apartment and see if it's still available. Depending on the outcome, I'll put down a first month's rent."

"How soon does he want you?"

"As soon as possible."

"Whoa. Are you ready to plunge in?"

"You can't imagine how excited I am to get started on my career."

"Well, I couldn't be happier. Mamma and Papa will be over the moon for you."

"I know. I need to call them now. Love you. Talk to you soon."

Scuol, Switzerland, July 28th

"Hey, buddy."

The dog lifted his head from the blanket, making a welcoming sound. But he didn't jump off the end of the bed and run to Vincenzo like he used to do.

With a heavy heart Vincenzo walked over to him and wrapped his arms around him. "You feel horrible, don't you? You're not alone," he murmured. "Forgive me for leaving you on your own for part of this Thursday. I had an official duty to perform and couldn't take you with me. We'll go visit Daniel first thing in the morning. He'll know how to help you."

The vet *had* to do something. Vincenzo knew that his dog, an unfailing source of love and devotion over the last seven years, was on his last leg. But he couldn't imagine losing him, not yet.

His dog watched him while he got ready for bed. As he was throwing on a robe, his cell phone rang. Vincenzo assumed it was either his mother or his younger sister Bella. He loved and missed her. She was away on vacation with her best friend Princess Constanza in Lausanne, Switzerland. But she loved their dogs too and worried about Karl. Vincenzo was anxious to talk to her, but when he went to click on, he saw the caller ID.

A call from Prince Rinieri Baldasseri of San Vitano, the second cousin he loved, came as a surprise. He worried that something else could be wrong with him since his tragedy and clicked on. "Rini?"

Instead of hearing him speak Romansh, Rini broke out in fluent Italian and didn't stop. Vincenzo was fluent in both as well as German and English. His cousin sounded so incredibly happy, he sank down on the side of the bed in shock.

After Rini had first gone missing presumed dead and then lost his memory in an earthquake last month only speaking Romansh, it was nothing short of a miracle to hear him sound and act like the old Rini.

"Hold on, Rini. Run all this by me again. Slower this time. Explain to me what's happened since we last spoke."

"My world has changed! Luna asked me to take her to Venice. When the fireworks went off, I'd been asleep and thought I was back in the mine when the earthquake hit the area. I jumped out of bed, needing to save the other miners. But before I could climb out the window, Luna grabbed me and held me back.

"She told me the booming sounds I heard were coming from the yearly fireworks show. After I could process everything, I suddenly realized I was with her. I also saw we were in the same hotel room we'd used during our honeymoon. Everything came back to me."

Beyond elated, Vincenzo got to his feet. "I'm overjoyed for you, Rini. I hear your euphoria and can't tell you how happy this makes me."

"I'm hoping to make you even happier. You don't have to act in my place any longer. I know how much you hated the whole idea of having to be King one day. So, *I'll* go on being the Crown Prince as if the amnesia had never happened. You're off the hook for something you never wanted in the first place."

"Thank heaven." Vincenzo closed his eyes for a moment over this news that had turned his life around once more in the most astounding way.

"*You*, my friend, can now get back to your life and your coming marriage. I spoke to the grandparents last night. They'll be forever grateful to you for stepping in when you did."

Vincenzo could scarcely contain his excitement. "I'll be on my knees to your wife for suggesting you go to Venice. Fireworks of all things. Who would have dreamed…?"

"None of us. And guess what else? We're going to have a baby!"

That meant the line of succession would go on with Rini's children. How wonderful for them. "You can't ask for more than that, you lucky dude. We'll talk again soon."

"Luna and I want you to bring your fiancée and come to dinner at the palazzo. I'll call soon to set a time."

"Sounds terrific." The two cousins had been close friends since childhood. "Welcome back, Rini. I've missed you."

"Ditto."

They both hung up. Vincenzo walked over to the dog in a daze and gave him another hug. Would that there might be one more miracle to transform his life. The engagement to Valentina Visconti had been his parents' horrendous idea from the start.

Vincenzo had never met Valentina and had only seen pictures of her in the news. Upon a first meeting a year ago, he knew he could never love her. The last thing he wanted to do was marry her. Vincenzo couldn't bear the thought of it, but it had been his father Marcello's dying wish.

Vincenzo's mother wanted the marriage at all costs too because Valentina came with the last name of the most powerful family in Italy. Of all the eligible princesses, his mother felt Valentina to be the grand prize, a fact she never let Vincenzo forget.

Marcello had been the second son of Alfredo Baldasseri, King Leonardo's brother, and had always felt a failure, never getting recognition, never measuring up. But in this one area where he could please the whole Baldasseri family and his wife, Marcello had exacted a deathbed promise from Vincenzo to marry Valentina.

The guilt had weighed heavily on Vincenzo to be the good son, something he couldn't ignore. Now that his father had passed away, his mother was determined he would follow through. She was close to irrational about it.

He knew in his gut Valentina didn't want to marry him either. When he'd said as much to her in the beginning, she'd played dumb and wouldn't admit anything. But he knew she was hiding something. At that point he realized she didn't dare fight her powerful father Stefano Visconti and Vincenzo knew why. Through him, Stefano was using his daughter to get at the Baldasseri timber fortune, a treasure the Visconti family coveted. His hold on Valentina was as binding as the vow Vincenzo's parents had forced out of him.

If only he could find a legitimate way to prevent the farce of the coming marriage…

Zernez, Switzerland, July 29th

Friday morning Daniel Zoller's eyes lit up when Francesca let herself in the back door of the veterinary clinic a few minutes before eight-thirty. The owner and head veterinarian of the Zoller Veterinary Clinic let out a sigh of relief. "Good. You're early. I have a patient in one of the examining rooms already. Dr. Peri is in another one. The bad news is, I found out our receptionist might be late coming in."

"Don't worry. I'll run the waiting room until Haida gets here."

"Bless you. I don't understand how we were so lucky you applied for the opening here. You've only been with us two weeks, and already I don't know what we'd do without you."

The warmth of the genius vet made him everyone's favorite whether they were a coworker or patient. She smiled. "I love being here and working with the legend. Thank you, Daniel."

As she'd learned earlier, the job required fluent Italian, English, German and a passable ability to speak Romansh. She'd thought the last would disqualify her, but Rolf hadn't let her be discouraged by her fears. Her brother had forced her to believe in herself.

Daniel had been so impressed with her credentials, he'd hired her anyway with the understanding she'd learn Romansh. Having vowed to learn the language of the people in the area, she'd been studying it on her off hours and practiced it everywhere she went.

The middle-aged doctor disappeared through a door that led to the main hall with examining rooms on either side. Twenty-four-year-old Francesca walked over to a closet and put on a fresh uniform. She fastened the knee-length light blue outfit with short sleeves and headed down the same hall to the front of the building.

After becoming a fully certified doctor of veterinarian medicine from the University of Milan, Italy, Dr. Francesca Giordano Visconti had investigated career opportunities. The one that had appealed most had been the opening here in Zernez. The village itself was a Tyrolean fantasy. To be working in the mountains where she could ski in winter and hike in summer thrilled her heart.

Francesca had found a great apartment and couldn't be more excited to do the work. She'd dreamed of being a vet since she was a little girl with a succession of dogs she'd treated like babies. Her parents had indulged her because she'd always loved animals and had been an outstanding student.

Excellent marks in academics had gotten her through high school early and she'd pushed ahead, graduating first in her class at the university. To her joy, that achievement had won Dr. Zoller's approbation.

Francesca couldn't be happier as she entered the reception room and sat down at Haida's desk. A list of scheduled appointments for the day would keep the clinic busy.

While she waited for the ten o'clock patient to arrive for a weekly checkup, she got on the computer to study a new list of Romansh vocabulary words. She heard voices as lab technicians and animal care workers had shown up to get busy. When the buzz of the front door sounded, Francesca lifted her head, then let out a quiet gasp.

It couldn't be—but it was.

Prince Vincenzo Baldasseri!

The Crown Prince of the Baldasseri royal family of San Vitano, a country on the Swiss/Italian border, had just entered the clinic. He'd come in with a medium-sized male Bernese Mountain Dog on a leash.

As she'd told Rolf, she'd known that the Prince's immediate family, including his beautiful sister Princess Bella, lived in the Baldasseri Palace in nearby Scuol, Switzerland, a village where the royals had been born and raised. He ran the timber business for the Baldasseri monarchy.

Still, Francesca couldn't believe what she was seeing. Over the last five years she'd watched various clips of him on the news. She'd also studied more videos on the nearby Biosphere Reserve since applying for the position here. The Prince had been featured in several of them where he explained his family's interest in preserving it for the future.

She'd thought the tall, dark, brown-haired royal had to be the most gorgeous man she'd ever seen in her life. In fact, she'd played the video several times, which was totally unlike her.

Though Francesca had dated here and there, she'd had no serious relationships. That would come later. School had been her priority. The idea of meeting and falling in love with a man as breathtaking as Prince Vincenzo would be pure fantasy.

Since he was engaged to her cousin, she was more than ever thankful she'd thought up a different last name and could use it. Estranged from the Visconti family before Francesca and Rolf had been born, her parents had moved to Bern, Switzerland. Her father had started a packaging business there that flourished. She and Rolf were total strangers to the other members of the Visconti family.

When she'd been hired for this vet position, she'd told her father she would be using a different last name. That way she could avoid notoriety as a Visconti while she worked in Switzerland near the Baldasseri royal family in Scuol. She'd been way ahead of her father's wishes on that score.

"Buongiorno," she called to the Prince.

He approached the desk with a look of worry on those hard-boned features that made him so handsome. "I haven't seen you here before." His deep male voice resonated to her insides.

"No. I'm new."

After studying her with an intensity that reached inside her, he said, "I don't have an appointment, but I need to see Daniel about my dog. Is he here?"

Everyone wanted Daniel. "He's in with another patient." She glanced at the wonderful dog with the tricolored coat who stayed near his master. He was the male version of her adorable Mitzi, another Bernese Mountain Dog she'd loved before leaving for medical school. "May I help you?"

"Thank you, but Karl is used to Daniel. How long do you think he'll be?"

"I have no idea. Maybe if you'd explain the problem to me?"

He checked his watch. No doubt he was in a hurry. "Karl has heart disease that causes him to cough and faint. But today I've brought him in because he now has a lump below his right eye. Is Dr. Peri here?"

"I'm sorry. He's with another patient. But I can try to help you. I'm Dr. Linard."

"*You're* a vet?"

Others had reacted the same way. She knew she looked young and obviously didn't have Daniel's experience. Heat swept into her cheeks. "I've only been here two weeks."

"Congratulations. You must have replaced

Dr. Zenger. Daniel wouldn't pick anyone to work here who isn't the best."

"Thank you but give me ten years and then tell me that again." An unexpected smile broke out on his face. The man's looks and charisma melted her to the floor. "Until Daniel can see you, why don't you bring Karl in the examining room and we'll take a look."

He nodded and they followed her down the hall to one of the rooms. She put her stethoscope around her neck, and checked him out. Karl indeed had a heart condition and wouldn't survive much longer. She leaned over to examine the dog's darling face. Memories of Mitzi assailed her. The Prince held on to him. She touched the lump and moved it around.

"That's very fleshy and could be an abscess." She looked up into the Prince's vivid blue eyes fringed with dark lashes staring at her intently. "Was he kicked or hit by something?"

"Not that I know of. It's been there for a while. I thought it would go away, but today I realized it has grown bigger."

"Hmm. How old is he?"

"About seven years now."

"Has the fainting grown worse?"

"It's been happening more and more after he exercises."

"I see." This breed had a life span of six to seven years. Francesca knew all about it. Her dog had died at six years while she'd been away at the university. She moved the lump again. "I don't feel a bone in it, so tell you what. In case it's an infection, I'm going to give him an antibiotic."

Francesca walked over to the corner where she kept her microscope and supplies. After filling the syringe, she returned to give him a shot. "Good boy. You handled that like a man." She bent down to ruffle his head and tickle him. To her surprise the dog licked her face the way Mitzi used to do.

The Prince chuckled. "He likes you. I haven't seen him do that to anyone but me."

"He knows I like him too." She stood up. "Take him home over the weekend and bring him back midweek. If it's worse, I'll open it up and take a look to see what's going on. But today we'll give him a break. We don't want Karl to be in pain, do we? Not when he's struggling with a bad heart." She patted him. This time he licked her hand. "You're a sweetheart."

"He feels the same about you," came the deep voice again. "When I bring him back, he won't have any problem letting you handle him."

His comments touched her. "We can hope," she teased with a smile.

"Tell Daniel I came by."

"I will. May I have your name?" As if she didn't know.

"Vince. He'll know who I am and bill me," he murmured and turned to leave with his dog.

Vince... So the Prince shortened his name. "*A revair*, Karl."

The Prince paused at the door. "You speak Romansh too?"

"I'm trying to learn it as fast as I can. In case your dog understands it, I hope he'll forgive me if my pronunciation needs more improvement."

Their eyes met. "I understand it too. You said it perfectly." His gaze swept over her. "Daniel knew what he was doing when he hired you, Dr. Linard."

With that compliment, he and Karl left the

room. As they walked toward the reception area, Francesca took in his casually dressed six-foot-three, rock-hard physique. Talk about an unforgettable man. As for Karl, the black-and-white dog with the rust markings couldn't be more adorable, bringing back memories of her own dog. How sad his life was coming to an end.

CHAPTER TWO

TWENTY-EIGHT-YEAR-OLD Prince Vincenzo Rodicchio Baldasseri walked out to his black Mercedes and lifted Karl into the rear seat. His dog looked back at the clinic through the window.

"You liked her, didn't you, buddy? Incredibly, so did I," he muttered to himself.

With the soft gold of her hair in a longish pixie-like style and those velvety brown eyes, she reminded him of an ornament of an enchanting fairy you saw hanging on a Christmas tree. There was a becoming flush on her cheeks. She was all fresh and sparkling. No ring on her finger. Her smile and knockout figure the uniform couldn't disguise had lit up his universe.

Lucky Karl had licked those enticing lips. That was the moment Vincenzo had needed to leave the room. He'd enjoyed his share of girlfriends before the engagement he'd been forced into by his parents' emotional blackmail. There'd been a few strong attractions, but nothing fatal. Yet even his sick dog had succumbed to Dr. Linard's spell.

She was a vet! Daniel, the best in Switzerland, had hired her. He chuckled that she'd said goodbye to Karl in Romansh. What other surprises were in store when he saw her again? He found he couldn't wait for the next appointment. But that's where his thoughts had to stop. The promise to his parents had turned his life into a living hell. It meant honoring it in every sense of the word.

The arranged engagement had been a union both royal families pushed hard for. On the surface Valentina acted willing enough, but deep down he knew she was only obeying her father's edicts. Thoughts of the coming wedding meant they would have to go through the rest of their lives in a marriage lacking the most important ingredient in order to make it work.

Bella had been sick for him. His childhood friend Luca Torriani groaned for him too. The three of them had been inseparable until the end of high school; then everything changed. These days he and Luca didn't often see each other though they stayed in touch. His friend had always known Vincenzo's deepest feelings about wishing he weren't being forced to marry a royal.

While he was lost in thought, his cell phone rang, startling him. He clicked on. "Mamma?"

"Finally. Why didn't you answer earlier?"

"I had to take Karl to the vet. How's Grandfather?"

"He's well enough. We heard from your great-uncle Leonardo in Asteria last night. You need to come home and explain to us what's really going on. What he told us makes little sense."

Of course! The two old brothers had already been on the phone. King Leonardo would have told Vincenzo's grandfather that Rini had recovered his memory and would end up being King one day instead of Vincenzo. They had to have discussed what his mother would consider to be a catastrophe in the Baldasseri family where Vincenzo was concerned.

Little did they know the astounding news

had overjoyed him, relieving him of the enormous burden he'd been carrying since the earthquake. The news that Rini was back better than ever would not only upset his mother, it had to have devastated Stefano. Vincenzo would phone Valentina to discuss it, but he needed to see about Karl first.

"I'll be there as soon as I can." He hung up and called his assistant Fadri. "Something urgent has come up. I won't be in the office today. Ring me if there's an emergency."

"Of course, Your Highness."

They hung up. Vincenzo turned on the engine and left the clinic's parking lot.

The half an hour drive back to Scuol took him past the three-hundred-year-old Baldasseri Timber Company. Full summer with all its color had come to the Engadin. He'd grown up in a timber family, learning every aspect of it. Timber had helped support the Baldasseri family both in Switzerland and in the country of San Vitano for three centuries. In the past, many a war had been fought over it, particularly with the Visconti family.

Vincenzo had headed the business since his father had passed away from a bad bout of flu a little less than a year ago. Being engaged had made it impossible for Vincenzo to live a bachelor existence any longer; therefore, he'd poured himself into the timber business to expand where he could and bring in more money to support his favorite causes.

Until his father's death, Vincenzo had been living in a town house in Scuol. Since then, he'd moved back in the palace to help with his grandfather who had to be on dialysis for his kidneys.

Soon he pulled into the courtyard and carried Karl up the staircase to the apartment of his grandparents, Prince Alfredo and Princess Talia Baldasseri. His mother was also there.

Both women sat by Alfredo's bed waiting for Vincenzo. The old man with thinning gray hair lifted his hand and waved it in greeting, but Vincenzo knew he felt miserable most of the time. His heart went out to him. He kissed the hand that had waved to him, then he brushed kisses on the cheeks of his grandmother and mother.

"Thank you for coming so quickly, son. We've had the most confusing news. It couldn't possibly be true."

Vincenzo put Karl down and pulled up a

chair close to them. "I'm afraid it is and I know all about it. Rini phoned me yesterday and we talked for a long time."

His sixty-three-year-old redheaded mother, Princess Maria Rodicchio Baldasseri, sat back in the chair as if in shock. "How can you be so composed after hearing such news? Why didn't you let us know the instant you hung up?"

"One question at a time, Mamma."

"Is it really a fact that your cousin no longer has amnesia?" his grandmother asked.

"Completely true, and I can't tell you how happy that makes me. Rini is back to normal. You should hear the joy in his voice. He and Luna are in ecstasy, especially since they're expecting a baby."

"Another heir?" his mother cried in despair.

"Mamma—it's all the greatest news anyone could have!"

Her body trembled in anger. "Is it the best news that you're *not* going to be the Crown Prince after all? It isn't right! Leonardo designated you to take over for him. He should behave like a true king and allow his word to stand."

"But Rini has regained his memory. It's *his*

right!" His gaze met his mother's and he saw the bitter disappointment in those blue eyes he'd inherited. "Rini is ready to do his duties again. He was always the perfect choice and the whole country is thrilled he didn't die in the earthquake."

"But, Vincenzo—"

"No buts, Mamma. An announcement will be made on the ten o'clock news tonight that he no longer has amnesia, that he'll go on assuming his duty as Crown Prince. Let's be grateful for the miracle that has happened to him. I know I am. Though I filled in for a brief time, it wasn't what I wanted to do. If I'm being truthful, I never wanted it," he murmured.

The thought of my coming marriage is anathema to me.

"How dare you say such a thing!" she cried. Her aspirations for him had always been over-the-top.

Vincenzo got to his feet. "I dare because I was never in line. One day Rini will make a great king. You know he will. He spent time here on vacations with our family. No one could replace him, certainly not me. Rini is the one to take over the kingdom when the time comes. That's his destiny, not mine."

Her skin grew mottled. "Your father would have been the perfect one to be King one day. If that flu hadn't taken my Marcello—" She couldn't finish her thought and broke down. He knew his mother still grieved for him. Nothing had been the same with his father gone.

"But Papa was never in line and Rini's father is dead. So is Rini's elder brother Paolo, who would have been named Crown Prince if he hadn't been killed at a young age. That left Rini and he's back to his old self. Face it, Mamma, none of it was meant to be for me. I was the last resort after the King thought Rini couldn't function, but no longer. With a baby on the way, the succession will be ensured."

"It isn't fair," she said in a withering tone. "I can't bear it."

"You've talked to Valentina?" his grandfather asked the important question.

"I'll call her in a little while."

His grandmother looked stunned, but said nothing. His mother buried her face in her hands. "This is going to come as the most terrible news imaginable to Valentina and the Visconti family."

Yes, Vincenzo mused. Valentina and her parents had expressed their joy that he'd been installed as the Crown Prince. To think that one day soon their son-in-law would become King of San Vitano; moreover, the Visconti family would hold valuable shares of timber stock they'd never been able to get their hands on. Those were huge considerations anticipated by that family.

But all that had changed now. His marriage would take place here in Scuol instead of the country of San Vitano. Without the incentive of Valentina being Queen one day, this latest news had to be a severe disappointment to her. But Vincenzo knew the real reason for the marriage. Stefano wanted to get his hands on the timber business. Valentina was the sacrificial lamb to accomplish it.

"I wish Bella were back from vacation," his mother moaned. "She's going to be terribly upset too."

No. Bella knew the truth of Vincenzo's feelings and would be thrilled he no longer had to perform that duty. She'd told him more than once that he should never have promised their father he'd marry Valentina. She'd thought it cruel of their mother to force their father to elicit that promise from him.

"If you'll excuse me, I'll go to my study and call Valentina. We need to talk before it's announced on TV and the newspapers. I'll check in with you again later."

The dog followed him out of the room and down the hall. Vincenzo didn't look forward to his conversation with Valentina who'd been caught up in the knowledge that one day she would be Queen. The day after Rini's reported death, Vincenzo had been informed that he was now the Crown Prince. When Rini was later found alive but having lost his memory, Vincenzo had had no option but to retain the title. Knowing that Leonardo's life was coming to an end, it appeared that becoming Queen was all Valentina could think about.

Her interest seemed to have grown into an obsession. That was because for reasons of her own, she hadn't wanted their arranged marriage. He imagined she thought that being Queen might compensate for what was missing between them. That's what came from not being in love. Who knew what her reaction would be when he got her on the phone?

Six o'clock in the evening rolled around at the vet clinic. Francesca splinted the dachshund's leg. She would love a dog, but it didn't pay to be in a rush when she'd barely settled here. Another few weeks and she'd find a darling dog to love and take care of. Her landlord had agreed she could have a pet. Of course, it would have to come to work with her, which meant she needed to discuss it with Daniel.

After the patient left, Francesca removed her uniform and put it in the laundry bin at the back of the clinic. Just then Daniel walked in. "How did it go today?"

"I had a surprise visitor named Karl."

He chuckled. "Vince's dog."

"Yes. He brought him in because Karl has a fleshy mass under his right eye. I could have opened him up, but instead I gave him an antibiotic and suggested he come back if it didn't get better."

The older vet nodded. "I'd have done the same thing. He's slowed down so much he's not going to be around soon. No point hurting him unnecessarily. His death will be a blow to Vince."

"The deaths of my dogs almost killed me."

"You lead with your heart. That's one of the reasons I hired you."

She admired this man so much. "Good night, Daniel. See you tomorrow."

On that note Francesca walked outside to her yellow Volkswagen and headed for her apartment in an eight plex. She lived on the second floor with a window box full of daisies outside her front room. En route she stopped to buy some groceries. She wanted something simple to fix and eat, like a ham omelet and toast.

After washing up, she cooked her meal and sat down on the couch to phone her parents. She owed them a call, but had been too busy until now. Her brother Rolf was finishing up his studies in Paris. Her parents had become empty nesters. They talked for a long time before hanging up, then she turned on the TV.

When the ten o'clock news came on, she found herself staring at a clip of Prince Rinieri Baldasseri. After meeting Prince Vincenzo this morning, what a coincidence to see his relative on the screen! The Baldasseri men were sinfully gorgeous.

A miracle has happened in San Vitano. Prince Rinieri Baldasseri, who lost his memory in an earthquake at the Baldasseri Gold Mine, has recovered it completely. To the joy of his grandparents, the King and Queen of San Vitano, today he has been proclaimed the Crown Prince once again. Congratulations to him and his wife, Princess Luna, who are expecting their first baby.

The Prince's second cousin Prince Vincenzo Baldasseri has been serving in that position and is also to be congratulated. No longer Crown Prince, he can attend to his duties full time as head of Baldasseri Royal Timber Enterprises in Scuol while he prepares for his nuptials to Princess Valentina Visconti of Milano, Italy.

Francesca turned off the TV, trying to imagine what it would have been like to have amnesia, then suddenly remember everything. Incredible. She got up and walked to the kitchen for a drink of water.

The news meant that Prince Vincenzo was no longer the Crown Prince. How did he feel about that? No doubt he'd have more time to prepare for his wedding.

As Francesca got ready for bed, she knew that if or when *she* ever got married, she planned to spend as much time with her husband as possible. Being the wife of a king would make it difficult to spend enough time together to suit her.

She considered it a plus for Valentina who was engaged to one fabulous man with a very sick dog.

Francesca's own parents had always been in love and enjoyed a close, wonderful marriage. She would never settle for anything less.

July turned to August. On Tuesday morning Francesca got busy vaccinating Mrs. Corsin's three healthy Bernese Mountain Dogs. The twelve-week-old pups were Francesca's favorite breed and too adorable for words, especially the one male she ended up cuddling. He licked her several times. His sweetness reminded her of Karl.

"What's the name of this one?" she asked the owner.

"Artur."

"Artur…" She spoke to him. "I could take you home with me." He was so cute.

"Do you have a pet, Dr. Linard?"

She put him in the crate. "Not since I moved here about three weeks ago, but it won't be long before I get one."

"I have a tentative buyer, but it might fall through. Would you be interested? Artur seems to have taken to you."

That did it. Francesca didn't hesitate. "I would love a call. I'll give you my number." When that was done she heard a knock on the door. Haida poked her head in. "Sorry to disturb."

"I'm just leaving." Mrs. Corsin gathered the crate with her puppies and left the room.

Haidi smiled at Francesca. "You have a patient waiting without an appointment."

"I'll be right out."

Her brows arched. "It's an *important* patient, if you get my meaning," she murmured with a glimmer in her eye before she hurried down the hall. Haidi was only a few years older than Francesca and a lot of fun.

The word *important* could only mean one thing. Francesca's heart ticked over in reaction, surprising her. She washed her hands and headed toward the front desk. The Prince sat in one of the chairs, studying something on his phone. Karl lay at his feet. When the dog's brown eyes saw Francesca, he made a sound and slowly got up.

"That's a wonderful greeting, Karl." She hunkered down to ruffle his fur and received another lick. "How are you feeling?"

"Not so well," his master responded and stood up. Once again the deep voice curled through her body, stirring her senses. Her gaze flicked to the Prince dressed in a tan crew-neck shirt and jeans that molded to his long, powerful legs. His dark wavy hair and hot blue eyes took her breath.

"I'm sorry to hear that." She patted the dog and got to her feet. "Come on. Let's go take a good look at you."

Karl followed on leash. When they reached the examination room, she lifted the dog's head and took another look at the fleshy mass. "You poor darling. I'm afraid there isn't improvement, so I'm going to open it up and see what I find." She eyed the Prince. "If you'll put him on the table and steady him, we'll get this over."

She noticed the play of muscle across the Prince's broad shoulders as he handled his dog with gentleness and care. You could tell a lot about a person's character by the way he treated his pet.

Francesca deadened the mass and felt around. "There's no bone or object in there. It appears to be sheer infection." She finished up the procedure and gave his dog another injection. Then she took Karl's vital signs.

"What's the verdict?" he murmured.

She lifted her head and their gazes locked. "I have to be honest, Your Highness. He—"

"Daniel *told* you who I was?" he interrupted.

"No. I've seen you on TV several times and on the videos featuring you discussing conservation efforts at the biosphere. Dr. Zoller suggested I watch the latest ones. I was going to say that Karl is in a bad way."

He studied her features for a moment, causing her chest to flutter. She wondered what he'd been thinking. "I know I should have put him down, but I can't bring myself to do it yet."

She heard his pain. "Since I've been through the experience with my own dogs growing up, I know what an agonizing decision that is. Take my advice and think about it a little longer, but not too long. You'll know when the time is right and you can't bear to watch him suffer any longer. Then phone the clinic. Whoever is on call will come."

He swallowed hard. "I want his passing to be peaceful, so I'll ask for you. I wasn't wrong the other day. He likes you." Everything he said was getting to her which was absurd. She'd met attractive men before; however, the engaged Prince was off limits in every conceivable way.

"Your dog is precious." Francesca fought to keep her voice steady and kissed his head. "See you soon, Karl."

The dog made a whimpering sound before his master picked him up. "Thank you, Dr. Linard. You have a special way."

She watched him carry his dog toward the front of the clinic. His hard-muscled silhouette with the dog in his arms was a sight she'd never forget.

The Prince remained in her thoughts all day. When your beloved pet wouldn't be on this earth much longer, the heart hung heavy. She knew what it felt like. Between memories of Mitzi and now Karl, she'd told Mrs. Corsin she'd buy Artur if he were available.

While Francesca fixed herself a salad for

dinner, she took a call from the brother she adored. "Rolf— What's new? Are the Parisian girls more exciting than Gina?"

"No way." He laughed. "Right now I'm working on my French and will tell you more *once* I can string a conversation together."

"I know what you mean. Romansh isn't the easiest language to learn."

"You were always a whiz at everything. I bet you're fluent already."

"Don't I wish. So what's new?"

"That's why I'm calling you. When I was home Sunday to see Gina, I heard the folks talking about some problem to do with the other side of the family that involved Valentina. They didn't realize I'd overheard them talking. Do you know anything about it?"

"Yes. It was on the news. Prince Vincenzo is no longer the Crown Prince of San Vitano."

"Yeah. The amnesia that Prince Rinieri suffered and recovered from is all the talk everywhere."

"Stefano is undoubtedly upset because Valentina won't be the Queen after all. That side of the family cares too much about titles. It's why Papa broke with them in the first place and has rejected all claims to his."

"Smart man, our father."

"I couldn't agree more, Rolf. Do you want to know a secret?"

"I'm all ears."

"You have to keep this to yourself. Swear you won't tell anyone?"

"I promise."

In the next breath she told him about Karl. "He's this wonderful Bernese Mountain Dog. Guess who he belongs to?" Then she told him.

Her brother whistled. "So *you're* the Prince's vet?"

"Daniel is his vet, but he had another patient so I took care of his dog. Amazing, huh. But the folks don't know, and I'll never tell them. It's a good thing I was prepared with a new name. A Romansh one at that, thanks to you."

"Funny how you were worried about this."

"I'm thankful the Prince doesn't have a clue I'm a Visconti or that I'm Valentina's cousin. He never will. So how is Gina?"

"We miss each other."

"I can only imagine."

"Hey—I've got to go. Do me a favor, Francesca. If you hear anything more from Mom and Dad about what's going on, call me. I can't help but be curious."

"That works both ways," came her honest response. "Ace those engineering tests, bro. Talk to you soon."

Francesca hung up and watched TV before getting ready for bed. After all these years she was amazed the subject of Valentina and her fiancé had come up at the same time Francesca had been treating his dog. The strange coincidence made it difficult for her to fall asleep. She especially couldn't put the picture of the Prince out of her mind. It alarmed her that he remained there through the rest of her work week.

CHAPTER THREE

BECAUSE OF BAD TRAFFIC on Friday after leaving Milano to see Valentina, Vincenzo arrived late in Scuol for a meeting with his personal solicitor and high-powered attorney Marko Fetzer. He hurried inside his private office at the Baldasseri Timber Company.

"Marko? Forgive me for not being on time."

"No problem, Your Highness. I haven't been waiting long. You said it was urgent."

"Extremely." He sat down in his leather swivel chair and eyed him. "This is about the papers you've been arranging for the transfer of a hefty percentage of Baldasseri timber stock to the Visconti account."

He nodded. "Everything is ready."

"I can always count on you. But there's been a change in plans. I want you to shred them."

The other man leaned forward in surprise.

"Is that because you have something else in mind?"

"No. The news I have to tell you isn't meant for another soul's ears yet."

"You have my word."

"I know that. The fact is, my engagement has been permanently called off."

The miracle he'd been praying for had happened. Valentina had accused Vincenzo of neglecting her over the last year, of not even pretending to be in love. He knew it was a ruse to cover what was really going on with her. Now that he wouldn't be King, there was no point to their bogus engagement and she had returned the ring he'd given her.

Vincenzo realized she too had been working on a way to get out of the sick alliance their parents had concocted. Hallelujah! The wedding wouldn't be happening! He was *free*! Stefano must be in a complete frenzy, but it was no concern of Vincenzo's.

Silence followed before Marko said, "I'm so sorry, Your Highness."

"Don't be. These things happen. I have no doubt it'll be announced on the news at some point."

If Marko only knew the joyous state of

Vincenzo's mind. He got to his feet. "Thank you for having taken the time to prepare the transfer. You're so good at what you do, expect another bonus for your service."

Now that their meeting was finished, Marko smiled and stood up. They shook hands before he left the office.

Vincenzo followed him out, anxious to get home to Karl. He'd left him in his mother's care. His dog's welfare and Dr. Linard's loving care were all he could think about as he drove to the palace and raced up the stairs to his own suite. Released from the ghastly vow he'd made to his father, Vincenzo could live again and intended to!

"Hey, buddy." He hunkered down to pet Karl who lay in his dog bed. He licked Vincenzo and moaned, letting him know he was glad he was back.

"I came as soon as I could." He kissed his head.

The sound of footsteps caused him to turn his head. "Mamma."

"Oh, good—you're back! Why didn't you come to Alfredo's bedroom? Your grandparents and I have been waiting hours to hear from you."

"I had to see Karl before doing anything else." And stop at the office for a vital private business transaction that would send Stefano into a new uproar. The timber stock was still out of his reach and always would be. "Has he eaten anything?"

"No, but he drinks every so often."

The condition of his dog had deteriorated since the last visit to Dr. Linard. "Thank you for watching over him. I'll carry him and we'll all talk."

With care he picked Karl up and walked through the palace to the suite where his grandfather was the most comfortable. Vincenzo sat down on the love seat with Karl next to him and ruffled his fur.

His grandmother flicked him a glance. "At last."

"Tell us everything, darling," his mother implored him.

Vincenzo's next words would bring the house down, but they had to be said.

"Valentina has called off the wedding."

"What did you say?" His mother jumped to her feet. "That's impossible."

"You heard me, Mamma."

"I don't believe it!" She looked shell-shocked,

but his grandmother said nothing. Vincenzo didn't understand her silence. That was strange.

"I do," Alfredo spoke up at once. "From the time the suggestion of a betrothal between Valentina and Vincenzo was proposed, they knew he was second in line for the throne. When Rinieri was injured and couldn't carry on as Crown Prince, that put my grandson at the forefront. They expected Vincenzo to become King."

Vincenzo thanked his grandfather silently. That was as good an excuse as any the older man could think of for her getting out of an engagement neither of them wanted.

"He still should be," his mother cried.

"No," Alfredo muttered. "Now that Rinieri is miraculously better and expecting an heir, Vincenzo is no longer a candidate. I'm afraid the disappointment was too much for them and Valentina."

Letting out a cry of pain, his mother left the bedroom. His grandmother followed. Vincenzo walked over to the bed and grasped his grandfather's hand. "You're right, Nonno."

Thank heaven the old man was a realist, even if he didn't know what was going on in Valentina's head. The problem was Vincenzo's mother. She'd grown way too attached to Valentina and was obsessed by her dreams for the two of them. Now the visions of the wedding and all it would signify in the years to come had gone up in smoke. Bella, on the other hand, would be thrilled for him. She believed in true love, period.

Dimmed gray eyes focused on him. "How are you handling this?"

"I'm fine, Nonno. I've already met with Marko and taken care of things."

"You were wise not to have the financial transaction take place until the day of the wedding. If I'm not wrong, you're much more worried about Karl than the woman you almost married."

"Nobody fools you," he murmured. Vincenzo patted his arm and stood up. "I need to have Karl put down, but I'm dreading it."

"Daniel will take care of it."

Yes, but Vincenzo didn't want the owner of the clinic to perform that service. Someone else had been on his mind for the last week giving him restless nights. He no longer had to feel any guilt about that. "What can I do for you before I see to Karl? Shall I ask Mother and Nonna to come back?"

"No. We need to give them time. Elsa will be bringing my dinner in a few minutes."

Elsa wasn't only a wonderful caregiver, she'd become his grandfather's friend. "I'll be in later to say good-night."

He walked over to the love seat. "Come on, buddy. Let's go back to my room and I'll ring for dinner. Afterward I'll let you sleep with me. How does that sound?"

An hour later he finished some business calls and phoned Luca with his news. His friend was overjoyed for him and agreed something serious and secret had to be going on with Valentina for her to break off the engagement with that neglect excuse. After they hung up, he was eating his dinner when his mother came in the suite. "We need to talk, Vincenzo."

"Please sit down. I know the news of our broken engagement has come as a blow to you."

"But not *you*?"

He walked over to the couch and put his arm around Karl. "If you want to know the truth—and I believe you'd prefer honesty between us—I'd like the kind of marriage you had with Papa."

"We were happy." His mother sank down in a chair. Her marriage to his father had been special.

"I never felt Valentina and I were right for each other, but for Papa's sake and yours I was willing to try and make it work. Now I don't have to."

"I knew you weren't enthusiastic, but I'd hoped you and Valentina would grow closer. She has to be devastated."

"Valentina wanted to be Queen, Mamma." Might as well use his grandfather's words. "In time her parents will find her another prince who will elevate her to the status she wants." He had no idea what Valentina really wanted.

His mother sat forward. "What we have to do now is arrange for a betrothal between you and Princess Constanza. You need to be settled with a wife, and I like her. If your father were still here, he'd insist on it." His mother had become much more overbearing since his father's death.

Vincenzo shook his head. "No more of that, Mamma. Rini met the love of his life and married her even though she was a commoner. He had the right idea. I'm no longer looking for a princess. When I meet the right woman and fall in love, I'll marry her."

"You can't mean that! I forbid it."

He burst into laughter. "Mamma—look what has happened. You and Papa tried your best for me by finding Princess Valentina, but it didn't work. I honored your wishes. Now I would like you to honor mine and accept how I feel."

"But Constanza has been crazy about you since she and Bella became best friends years ago. She's lovely and an heiress who would bring Lorchat Robotics Corporation with her."

"I like Constanza, but I'm not in love with her and never could be. It's out of the question. When the right nonroyal woman comes along for me, I plan to marry her."

She got to her feet. "Wait until your grandparents hear about this."

"You can talk to them, but no one will change my mind."

"Vincenzo? You're not thinking clearly right now," she said in an authoritative voice. "I'm going to leave you and we'll talk again tomorrow."

He walked her to the door and kissed her

cheek. "You need a good night's sleep, Mamma. Thank you for taking such good care of Karl today. That meant more to me than anything."

"He's been a remarkable dog. It pains me that he's gotten so old. But I'm more pained to think that you won't be marrying Valentina. I know you liked her. Don't forget that she's been in love with you for a whole year. Since you refuse to consider Constanza, I'd like to believe there's still hope for you and Valentina. This isn't over yet. Wait and see. Good night."

He shut the door behind her. His poor mother. She refused to see the truth and wasn't about to give up on her dream. No doubt she would try to think up an added incentive to win over Valentina and her family, but Vincenzo had news for her. Without the timber fortune, nothing else could make up for it with Stefano. Fortunately, Bella would be coming home from her trip soon. He needed an ally.

His gaze flicked to the loving dog who lay there without moving. It was time…

Daniel had worked out a schedule. Each vet would work at the clinic one Saturday a month, half day for emergencies. Francesca was just finishing up her Saturday duty before leaving at two when the last call came in at the desk. She picked up. "Zoller Veterinary Clinic—"

"Dr. Linard?"

Her pulse raced. She knew that deep voice. "Your Highness? How's Karl?"

"I think you already know." His mournful tone said it all.

"Why don't you bring him to the clinic. We're closing in a few minutes, but I'll stay and we'll take care of him."

"Thank you. I'm on my way."

Francesca clicked off, steeling herself not to give in to the sadness. She went to the examining room to prepare the IV that would relax Karl and put him to permanent sleep.

When everything was ready, she walked through the clinic and opened the front door. A glorious August day greeted her. She leaned against the framework with her arms folded across her waist. The Prince's image had been on her mind since the first day he'd come in the clinic with Karl. This would be his last visit. She should be glad because her attraction to him was too strong and pure insanity.

Francesca started to turn away when she saw his black Mercedes approach. As she watched his tall, fit body get out and carry a limp Karl toward her, sadness crept through her. Pain lines defined the Prince's unforgettable male features.

"*Bun di*, Karl," she murmured good morning in Romansh and kissed the top of his head. He lifted it a trifle, but not enough to lick her. "Follow me." She walked ahead of them until they reached the designated room.

Vincenzo laid him on the table. He leaned over. "You're with friends, Karl." His dog moaned as if he understood completely.

Her gaze collided with the Prince's mournful eyes. "If you'll steady him, I'll administer the dose in his back leg. It'll relax him and send him into sleep."

"This is it," he whispered. His grief reached inside her.

"Yes, and the best way. Merciful. When you two are in heaven together one day, he'll thank you."

"You believe that?" he whispered.

"I'm planning on being reunited with all

my pets. My latest dog, Mitzi, had to be put down while I was away at medical school. I plan to see her again one day."

Tears had filled those incredibly blue eyes. He looked down. "It's okay, buddy."

The dog didn't stir as Francesca inserted the IV. She stared at Karl. "You're going to have the most wonderful dreams. You'll be running and chasing everything in sight. You'll be joined with other dogs who will be there to play with you. Your life is just beginning, darling Karl."

Within a minute and a half, he was gone. She knew the Prince needed time alone with him, so she left the room and went out to the desk to wait.

He appeared ten minutes later, his eyes still moist. She looked up at him from the computer.

"Karl passed without any trauma. That's because he knew he was in the hands of an angel," he told her.

"Thank you, but you gave him the constant love in his life. Do you want an urn with his ashes delivered to the palace?"

"No. I have pictures and videos to remember him."

"My sentiments exactly."

After a pause, "Dr. Linard, when will you be off work?"

Her pulse sped up for no good reason. Why did he want to know that? "In fifteen minutes." She needed to take care of Karl.

"Do you have plans for the rest of the day?"

She blinked. "Only to go home and get some housework done."

"If I come by then, would you be willing to take a drive with me to Karl's favorite spot where he loved to chase around?"

The invitation thrilled her to the core of her being, but it was out of the question. "Surely your fiancée, Princess Valentina, will want to go with you." Francesca would never consider it.

"I'm afraid not. Our engagement has been called off permanently."

Permanently? She reeled. *He wasn't marrying her cousin? What was going on?*

The news surprised her for several reasons she didn't dare examine. "I'm so sorry, Your Highness."

He shook his dark head. "It was an arranged engagement that didn't work out."

What? She had so many questions, but

couldn't ask one. "Still, this must be a painful day for you."

"Learning about *your* dog, only you could understand my feelings at the moment." His emotions stirred hers. "Will you come with me?"

She could hardly breathe, let alone refuse what her heart wanted. "I'd love to. I bet Karl will be there wondering what took you so long."

A compelling smile broke out on his handsome face. "Imagine his joy when you show up with me."

CHAPTER FOUR

Fifteen minutes later Dr. Linard left the clinic and walked to Vincenzo's car carrying her purse. The sun gilded her hair. Without her uniform, her feminine curves looked fabulous in jeans and a short-sleeved print blouse. She had to be five foot five. Her beauty electrified him.

He got out. "Why don't I follow you to your home, and we'll go from there."

"Luckily I live here in Zernez."

"Perfect. Don't mind my security people trailing us. They go where I go."

She smiled and walked over to a yellow Volkswagen. He loved her choice of car and enjoyed trailing her to the apartment complex with flower boxes where she lived.

"I'll run in and be right out."

"No hurry," he called to her. He noticed

she lived on the second floor. When she returned, he opened the front passenger door for her and they were off. Her flowery fragrance wafted past him.

"Where are we going?"

"To the mountains outside Scuol about ten minutes from here."

"What made them so special for Karl?"

"He liked to find ground-nesting birds and bark at them. His favorites were several families of skylarks and corncrakes hiding in the grass."

She smiled. "I never did hear him bark."

"He loved scaring them."

Francesca's laughter infected him. "I can only imagine how much you're going to miss him. He had the sweetest disposition."

"I never had a dog like him."

"You're lucky he was able to live with you to the very end. I told you about Mitzi. She was a Bernese Mountain Dog like Karl. I was away at school and didn't get to say goodbye to her."

He took in her profile. "I'm sorry about that. Our pets mean a lot."

"You're right about that."

"Where did you study?"

"In Milano."

All the time she was in school there, his former fiancée lived in the same city. But it was no good to think about the "what-ifs."

Vincenzo took a turnoff and the car climbed to a higher elevation. He parked at a vista overlooking the familiar alpine scenery and turned off the engine.

"What a beautiful sight!" She turned to him. "This is heaven. Can you see Karl yet?" Her warm brown- eyes twinkled. The sad day was turning out to be something else.

"Why don't we try to find him?" he teased.

"You're on."

They both got out and followed a path that led to some trees. "Karl would sit here and wait until he heard the low buzz-like call of the corncrakes."

Her eyes wandered over him. "Will I know it if I hear it?"

This playful woman was getting to him. "Let's find out." They both sat on a log where Karl would sit at his feet.

Different kinds of birdsong filled the air while they listened. After five minutes the funny buzz sounds rent the air. She jumped up with the joy of a child. "I heard it!"

Nothing got past her. He stood up. "You certainly did. Maybe Karl is spooking them for you."

"Oh, I hope so!"

They stood there together smiling into each other's eyes and waited. Pretty soon they heard more on-and-off buzzes. A couple of the little birds scuttled through the grass. "Karl's after them, all right."

She looked up at him, her face glowing. "Thank you for bringing me here. The second I heard your voice on the phone earlier, I knew the reason. But being here where you said Karl loves to play has relieved much of my sadness."

His eyes darkened. "Mine too."

"From now on I'll think of him up on this mountain having the time of his life. I love the mountains too."

He didn't want this day to be over. "How would you like to get a bite to eat on our way back?"

"That sounds good. I skipped lunch because of the shorter day."

"I couldn't eat anything today, but now I find I'm hungry."

"Understood."

Vincenzo drove them to Zernez, asking her more about her work with Daniel. He stopped at a drive-through for ham-and-cheese croissants, which they both enjoyed.

Much as he'd wanted to take her to a restaurant, he didn't want to create publicity until the news of his broken engagement had circulated and died down. For now, this kind of excursion would have to do. Despite saying goodbye to Karl, he couldn't remember the last time he'd been this relaxed and happy. She'd made all the difference.

Once he'd driven her to the apartment complex, he shut off the engine and turned to her. "I want to thank you for helping me get through this day."

"To be honest, it helped me too," came her unexpected response without looking at him. "I find I'm attached to all my patients, especially ones that look like my last dog. Karl headed the list. Daniel says I need to toughen up, but I have a feeling there's no cure for it."

Every word out of her mouth enchanted him. He had to see her again. "Since you told me Daniel asked you to watch some videos on the Biosphere Reserve, I thought you might be interested in meeting the biologist who used to work with Dr. Zenger. The conservation board is meeting Tuesday evening at the information center here in Zernez. The chief ranger of the park will be speaking."

"I would absolutely love it!" she exclaimed without hesitation. "I was envious when Daniel told me Dr. Zenger helped take care of some of the animals up there. What time does this meeting start and I'll drive over."

"Seven o'clock. The information center consists of three buildings. The meeting will take place in the Planta-Wildenberg castle. I'll look for you there."

"Thank you so much for giving me the opportunity, and for the dinner." She started to get out of the car.

"It was my pleasure. See you there."

He waited until he could see she was safely inside her apartment, then he left for home with a new excitement. Only three more days before he saw her again.

When Tuesday arrived, it dragged on. After talking to a couple of plant managers who had complicated problems, Vincenzo took off for Zernez later than he'd intended.

Dr. Linard had arrived ahead of him. She was surrounded by mostly male members of the board in the small conference room. Gian Mattlis, the head biologist, was talking animatedly with her. No surprise there. She looked fabulous in a peach-colored two-piece suit with short sleeves.

"Your Highness," one of the reserve authorities greeted him. "We've been getting acquainted with Dr. Zenger's replacement at the Zoller clinic. Dr. Linard is a very welcome addition."

The grin on the chief ranger's face revealed his interest too. "I'm going to take her up where I can guarantee she'll see some ibex and chamois."

Vincenzo's gaze flew to those chocolate orbs of hers. "That ought to be a great adventure, Dr. Linard."

Her gentle smile connected. "I'll look forward to it."

The president of the board called the meeting to order. "Now that His Highness is here, we can get started."

Vincenzo walked over to her. In high heels she stood a little taller. The perfect size for him. "Shall we take a seat?" He found two on the first row for them.

After a reading of the minutes of the last meeting, it was the ranger's turn to talk. "We need to be concerned about the laws that have been applied in the reserve. Are they doing the job?

"To review what we know about the ibex, if you kill the wrong animal, you pay a fine and get nothing. Heaven forbid if you shoot the animal and leave it wounded, which is where Dr. Linard comes in. Naturally you lose your license.

"At present, the reserve here in Graubünden is only allowing locals to hunt the ibex for a very short window in time." He read some statistics. "We don't want them to make the endangered species list. Before you leave this meeting, please write your suggestions about the rules and put them in the box here on the desk."

The ranger played the most recent video they'd made about the biosphere. Vincenzo noticed Dr. Linard appeared enchanted as they watched the flourishing wildlife in the upper elevations. He preferred taking in her reactions and counted the minutes until it ended and they could leave to be alone.

"Are you hungry? I left straight from work, and now I'm starving. After I follow you home, let's get something at the drive-through."

"You're reading my mind."

Her answer meant she wasn't ready to say good-night yet. He picked her up in front of her apartment and they decided to go for meat pies. From there he drove her to a nearby park and turned off the engine so they could eat.

"Um... This is delicious, Your Highness."

"I agree."

She glanced at him. "I noticed you didn't write any suggestions in the box."

"That's because the board already knows my feelings," he explained.

"Which are?"

"I'd rather there was no hunting at all in the reserve. I'd love to leave it as pristine as the day it was created."

Her eyes played over his features. "You really mean that, don't you?"

"Yes. There's a time and a place to hunt, but centuries ago wise stewards wanted to create the place we now know as the Biosphere Reserve. A place untouched by man."

"That's a thrilling concept and gives me gooseflesh just thinking about it. The idea of those beautiful animals being wounded kills me."

"I felt the same way the first time I hiked there. My friend Luca and I found a baby ibex in serious trouble. It lay against its mother who'd been shot and was dying. We took it to the vet and it recovered, but that incident did it for me."

"I admire you more than you know for doing all you can to preserve nature this way."

"I'm afraid I face a lot of opposition. Trophy hunting is lucrative."

"Many bad things are, but you're still willing to do something about it. I feel honored that you made it possible for me to be there tonight. Just so you know, your fight is mine."

Where had this adorable woman come from? He started the car and took her back to her apartment. "Don't be surprised if the chief ranger gets in touch with you to take that hike and other things. He didn't look that happy when you left the room."

"I saw his wedding ring, so if he calls, I'll let him know I would never spend time alone with a married man."

With whom *did* she spend time? "Tell me—is there someone important in your life?"

She looked away. "Not yet."

How could that be? "Are you enjoying your work?"

"Being a vet is all I could ever want, but I'm not doing so well learning Romansh."

Vincenzo smiled. "Karl understood you."

"He was a genius. It's harder than I thought."

"That's because nobody speaks the standard form except possibly some news announcers. I think you've already figured out it's a conglomeration of dialects. I've sorted through dozens of them and they each have their own grammar."

"Can you speak every dialect?"

"I'm not Karl. I suggest you try to pick up one. At least then when you speak it, you won't sound phony."

"Have I been sounding phony?"

One brow lifted. "The truth?"

"Oh, no—" Color rushed into her cheeks. "What must Daniel think?"

Vincenzo burst into laughter. He couldn't help it. She ended up laughing with him. He loved it that she didn't take herself seriously. "You know exactly what he thinks or he wouldn't have hired you. Between you and me, he knows it's impossible to master. The fact that you promised to try had to have delighted him."

"You always make me feel good. Thanks for everything this evening, Your Highness. Good night." She got out of the car before he could come around. Soon she reached the second floor and waved to him. There was no woman in the world with a personality as charming as hers. That's when it hit him.

He wanted to be with her all the time.

Around noon Sunday, Mrs. Corsin called Francesca to tell her one of the puppies was available if she still wanted it.

Francesca said she'd love to buy it. Mrs. Corsin planned to bring the puppy to the clinic on Thursday when she was in town for another appointment. A new dog would keep Francesca busy so she wouldn't think about Prince Vincenzo anymore.

Being with him at the information center and their talk afterward hadn't been a good idea. During the time they'd been together, she'd forgotten he was a prince. They'd laughed and shared some special moments in such a natural way, she hadn't wanted the evening to end.

Later in the day her mother phoned, giving her news she'd already heard from the Prince. So much for putting him out of her mind. "Your father has been told through certain sources that there'll be no marriage between the Visconti and Baldasseri families. Word is that Stefano is in a fury."

Francesca took a deep breath. The Prince had told her the called-off engagement had been arranged. That personal information wasn't public knowledge. This wasn't a conversation she should have with anyone, not even her mother. "I'm sure both families are upset, Mom."

"Your dad is certain the plans were called off because Prince Vincenzo is no longer the Crown Prince."

"Probably." It was time to change the subject. "How are you two?"

"Missing you. How's work?"

"I love it, and guess what. I'm buying a dog."

"That doesn't surprise me. What breed?"

"It's a male Bernese Mountain Dog, twelve weeks old and adorable. Three puppies were born. I inoculated them and fell in love with one that snuggled against me and licked me."

Laughter came from her mom. "Your dad will be delighted to hear it. We wondered how long you could last without one."

"Not long apparently. After he has settled in, I'll take pictures of him on my phone and send them to you."

"Do you have a name for him already?"

"Yes, it's the one the owner gave him. Artur."

"How cute!"

"He's named after her favorite pianist, Arthur Rubinstein."

"*Arturrr*... I love it."

"It's perfect, and now I've got to buy some stuff before the store closes so I'm ready by Thursday when I bring him home."

"He'll be the happiest pup on earth living with the sweetest girl in the world."

"I love you, Mom. Give Dad a hug from me."

Late Monday afternoon Daniel asked Francesca to come to his office before she left. As she stepped inside still in her uniform, it stunned her to see Prince Vincenzo sitting there in a gray suit and tie. He got to his feet, possessing a male virility she couldn't ignore.

His intense blue eyes focused on her. "Dr. Linard?"

"Your Highness."

"I'd hoped to catch you before you went home. Please, sit down."

Francesca sank into the other chair, far too excited over their visitor to do anything else and angry about his effect on her.

"I was telling Daniel that you were a hit at the last board meeting. I've had several calls from the members about you. They feel that with your background as a vet, you would be a great spokesperson for our cause."

"That's very kind, but I'm a novice barely out of veterinary school."

He shook his dark head. "According to Gian Mattlis, your philosophy about preservation of the species impressed him so much, he's hoping you'd be willing to narrate part of our next video for the reserve. He'd like to do it next month. Since it will have to be filmed on a weekday, I wanted Daniel's permission before approaching you."

"Which you have." Dr. Zoller smiled at her.

Francesca stirred uncomfortably in the chair. "I'm honored by your confidence in me, Your Highness, but I couldn't do something like that, let alone in front of a camera. It's not me."

The Prince's gaze fused with hers. "What happened to, 'your fight is mine'?" Guilt smote her. "Will you at least let me give you a small tour to see the reserve before you decide you can't do it?"

"Of course, she will," Daniel answered for her.

"I was thinking tomorrow if that's at all possible."

Daniel nodded. "It will be no problem for her to be gone for the day."

Francesca's boss knew why she didn't want to get involved, so why wasn't he helping her get out of this? "If you're sure, Daniel."

"Preserving the integrity of the reserve is of paramount importance. As your employer, I'm pleased for you to be included."

"It would please *me* no end, Dr. Linard." Those electric blue eyes mesmerized her.

"Very well. I'm honored that you'd take me on a little tour."

The Prince got to his feet with a look of satisfaction. "I'm due at the palace now. Plan for me to come to the clinic at eight thirty in the morning for you."

"I'll be ready."

After he left the office, Dr. Zoller cocked his head. "You've been bestowed a personal compliment by the Prince himself."

"I realize that, but I would have preferred not to get involved."

"We both know you wanted to turn him down because you're a Visconti, but maybe it will never be necessary. Remember, he's no longer engaged to your cousin. His association with that name has been dissolved and I've never seen him happier in my life. There will be other women. Give it a little more time before you decide you have to reveal your secret to him."

Daniel did have a point, but Francesca had the feeling he knew a lot he wasn't telling. The two men had been friends for years. She got to her feet. "This isn't the best time for me. I'm just getting started on my career and I'm buying a dog. It's more than enough."

His hands parted. "If you really feel that way, I can contact him today and tell him you aren't interested after all. Naturally it's your decision."

"No. Please don't do that. I said I would. See you in the morning, Daniel."

CHAPTER FIVE

FRANCESCA LEFT THE clinic and drove home. The thought of a whole day with the Prince out in nature filled her with an exhilaration she didn't know how to contain. What to wear?

She spent a restless night waiting for morning to come. After some deliberation she dressed in jeans and a new khaki shirt with roll tab sleeves and a collar.

When she reached the clinic, she saw a van with the Biosphere Reserve logo parked in the lot. As she parked and got out of her car, she saw this tall, hunky male walking toward her in jeans and a dark green pullover. Good grief. With that dark hair and those cobalt eyes, no better-looking man had ever been born.

"*Bun di*, Dr. Linard," he said in Romansh. "Right on time. I'm glad because it's a beautiful day and we've a lot to see. Have you eaten breakfast?"

"I did, and presume you did too. Thank you."

"Do you have to go inside the clinic first?"

He was almost rocking on the heels of his hiking boots, exactly the way her brother did when he was eager to escape to somewhere. "I'm ready to leave now, Your Highness."

"Then let's be off. I've brought treats, water and a picnic, so we shouldn't be in want of anything."

Francesca knew this man had thought of everything. He was what every man should be, let alone a prince.

They walked over to the passenger side of the van and he helped her in. His hand accidentally brushed against her leg. It sent darts of sensation through her. Oh, boy. Already aware of him, his touch threw her into a new, deeper kind of trouble.

"We'll drive to the right side of the Inn River and continue driving to the three-thousand-meter level to take in the view. Italy isn't far away from there."

She eyed him. "I have a confession to make. In medical school, my professors sang

Dr. Zoller's praises. Their remarks made me want to see if I could work there with him after graduation. Until I looked at a map, little did I know this biosphere reserve was located so close to the clinic. Since I've always loved the mountains, the proximity turned out to be a dream come true."

"I can understand your delight," he said. "The reserve is a magnet for nature lovers. Most of them are hikers who have to stay on the marked trails—however, some of the trails are off-limits in high summer, but we can drive to places I want you to see."

"This is a privilege I would never have expected, Your Highness."

He grinned. "Stick with me and see the wonders of the world."

She needed to stop staring at his handsome face or she'd have a heart attack. "You grew up surrounded by mountains."

"Yes. They've been the playground for my sister Bella and me. When we were young, our mother didn't like us spending so much time away from the palace. We did it anyway in order to hike and try to catch fish with nets."

"How funny!"

He smiled. "It was fun too. In our teens we managed to sneak away after dark and camp out some nights until our parents found out."

"Uh-oh."

"Uh-oh is right. At that point everything was brought to a halt."

"You mean you had to grow up."

Their eyes met and she saw a sadness enter his that hadn't been there before.

"Afraid so."

"Now you have your duties."

Like Francesca's father, who had walked away from his to marry her mother. But she couldn't talk about that with the Prince.

Francesca looked out the window. She decided to stop worrying about everything and simply enjoy this trip. Having been invited by the Prince of the Engadin gave her a coveted entrée here. Being with him made her world feel magical.

"What about you, Dr. Linard? Do you have siblings who got into trouble with you?"

She laughed. "My brother Rolf made up for half a dozen adventurous brothers and sisters. He's a rascal, but I adore him."

"How old is he?"

"A year younger than I am. Right now he's

finishing his engineering studies in Paris. When we were young, our parents took us to Chamonix, France, every winter where we skied to our hearts' content. Those mountains became our favorite place. You probably love to ski."

"Whenever I get the chance—however, there was a time when I worried I wouldn't be able to do much of it."

"Why was that?"

"My great-uncle Leonardo designated me to be the Crown Prince after my cousin Prince Rinieri came out of that earthquake with amnesia."

"What a terrible experience that must have been for him."

"It was a nightmarish time for him and for me. It meant responsibilities I didn't want to take on, *and* I had to cut down on my skiing." She laughed. "Luckily he recovered his memory."

"I don't blame you for how you felt. I can't imagine anything worse than being a king. It makes me shudder just to think about it."

"Do you really feel that way?"

"Absolutely. You don't have free agency when you're born into a royal family, but now I'm being rude to you. I'm sorry. I had no right to say that." Her father's struggle to become his own person would always live with her.

"Please don't apologize, Dr. Linard. I enjoy your frank speaking. It's more refreshing than you know. No wonder Daniel thinks the world of you. In case you didn't know, he's happy you applied."

"It's mutual, believe me. Do you know I almost missed the experience of meeting and working with him?"

"Why?"

"When I was searching for the right veterinarian opening six weeks ago, you can bet I looked for a good one in Chamonix."

"But nothing could compare with working for Daniel," he interjected.

"He's known everywhere, and I've discovered he's a remarkable doctor."

"Amen to that."

Over the next little while they passed grasslands, meadows, forests, all the elements of nature that caused people to flock to Switzerland's grandeur. Visitors were out en masse. He handed her a pair of binoculars. "If you'll look over on that crest, you may see some sights people spend thousands of dollars hoping to glimpse."

The Prince was loving this. So was Francesca, more than she would have ever dreamed possible.

She kept scanning the top of the crest and soon she saw movement. "Oh—there's a tan chamois! Your binoculars are so powerful, I can tell it has dark legs and two horns. It looks like a goat, only bigger."

He nodded. "More like an antelope?"

"Yes. It's beautiful! How wonderful we have creatures like this. I love it that you and your family have fought to preserve places where we can see them outside of a zoo."

"I suppose a zoo has its place, but there's nothing like the great outdoors."

They kept climbing higher.

All of a sudden, she cried, "There are two red deer and further on an ibex!"

His deep chuckle sent delicious chills through her body. "You've hit the jackpot today. Many are the times when you don't catch sight of an animal. Today they've come out for you."

The things he said...

He pulled the van to the side of the road

and parked. "I'll get us something to eat and drink." Quick as a shot he got out and opened another door to grab some items. Once in front again, he handed her a water bottle and some Cailler Swiss chocolate.

"How did you know this is my favorite?"

His brows lifted. "Isn't it everyone's?"

They both laughed before she handed him the binoculars. "Your turn." She started eating several squares of chocolate. Heaven.

"Another Ibex has appeared. It must be its mate. They're having a great day just like we are."

Francesca averted her eyes. Every moment, every word with him was making this outing unforgettable.

"I'm going to drive higher. Who knows what we'll find?"

After putting the binoculars around his neck, they headed out again. She didn't spot any hikers at this point. "We won't see brown bears, right?"

"No."

"That's too bad. I love to watch them."

"They've been extinct since 1904, but some time ago a young bear did migrate here. It was a male and no population will develop without a female. I presume we'll see more from time to time."

"How do you feel about allowing them here?"

"They would be good for tourism though there is pressure against it in some sectors. I welcome them as long as we put appropriate safety measures like fencing in place. Brown bears are pretty shy."

"They're part of the whole animal world up here," she added. "I like the idea very much."

He sent her a sideward glance. "You see? You'd be perfect to help us do the next video, but I won't say another word about it. That will have to come from you."

Clever man to bring her here. Who could refuse this Prince who charmed her down to her toenails?

When they came to the edge of a forested area, he pulled off the road once again. "Time for lunch. We'll sit on the fallen tree over there and enjoy the eastern view of the Piz Pisoc."

Pockets of snow filled its mountainous crags. "What can I bring?"

His eyes glowed a burning blue. "Yourself."

Heat radiated through her. They both got out and he pulled a cooler from the back. She followed his fit body over the grass. A few yards into the forest and they reached the fallen tree. He lowered the cooler and opened the lid. Two plates had already been prepared with food and he handed her one which she uncovered.

"This didn't come from the deli in town. It's a feast."

A chuckle escaped his throat. "My favorite cook at the palace made this meal for us."

"How am I so lucky?"

"Because you're with me." She loved his teasing. "I did stop at the deli for soda. I hope you like Pepita."

"I drink it quite often." She leaned down and reached for one that was chilling on ice. They ate in companionable silence for a few minutes, but she still felt terrible for what she'd said to him.

"Your Highness? Please forgive me for being so outspoken to you a minute ago. I can't believe I did that. No one has ever been kinder or more wonderful to me."

His eyes glinted. "Are you saying you're

sorry enough to help with the video we'll be working on next month?"

"After what I did, I'm putty in your hands. Oh, dear—" She felt herself blush. "That's the wrong thing to say too. I'm so embarrassed."

A deep laugh poured out of him, disturbing some white-bellied alpine swifts clinging to the side of a nearby tree.

They finished eating and he packed everything up to take back to the van. "If you're ready, I'll drive us to a spot where we might see an old married couple I'd like you to meet."

Her eyes widened. "What are you talking about?"

"You'll see," he murmured. "At least I hope they'll show up."

He had her intrigued as they climbed to the summit where he slowed down. "Look to the right." She did his bidding. "What do you see?"

"No people."

"I'm talking about the old married couple. Look again." He handed her the binoculars.

She put them to her eyes. It took her a minute to cover everything. "All I see are two birds with large wingspans cruising around."

"Not just any birds, Dr. Linard. They're golden eagles, hunting for marmots. I've hiked close to their eyrie many times. Their marriage has lasted longer than those of some humans."

Francesca shook her head in amazement. "How wonderful! What a fantastic sight! I wouldn't have missed it." She turned toward him. "Thank you so much for bringing me here. I'll always treasure this day."

His compelling smile illuminated her insides. "It's been my pleasure and I'm sorry we have to head back to the clinic."

So am I...so am I.

They turned around and talked about the forthcoming video while they made the breathtaking descent. The last thing she wanted to do was leave this land of enchantment that included a man she couldn't believe existed, a man who... Her thoughts had to stop right there.

He handed her some more chocolate and her bottle of water, always looking out for her. She was desperate to find any faults in him. So far she hadn't found one. Her only problem was that she'd been born a Visconti, the natural enemy of a Baldasseri.

At quarter to five in the evening they pulled into the clinic parking area. The Prince drove the van over to her car and helped her get out. "When arrangements are made, I'll be in touch with you about filming the video next month. Now I'm due back at the palace."

"Of course." Emptiness filled her to realize it would be a whole month before she talked to him again. "Today's tour made me appreciate the great value of the biosphere. It thrills me to be a tiny part of something so important." She opened her car door. "*Buna sera*, Your Highness."

Vincenzo went into work early the next two days, anxious to get busy making up for being gone the day before. Over lunch on Thursday he took a call from his mother. Bella would be home from vacation today. At dinner his mother planned to discuss what he was going to do to fix the situation with Valentina. His poor deluded mother. He told her they'd talk later.

At four thirty he left for the vet clinic. By the time he arrived there, it would be the end of Francesca's working day. She was constantly on his mind. He'd never been so entertained in his life, nor as attracted, and couldn't wait a second longer to see her. Thoughts of her finally being willing to help make the video had brightened his mood.

The receptionist smiled up at him. "Prince Vincenzo?"

"I know I don't have an appointment, but I need to see Dr. Linard. Is she available?" Her car was still in the parking area.

"She's with a client, but I'll walk back and tell her you're here."

"Thank you."

As he stood there, a woman carrying an empty crate came through. She stared at him for a moment. It happened wherever he went. Vincenzo would never know the meaning of anonymity. He greeted her before she left the clinic.

The receptionist came back. "Dr. Linard will be with you in a moment." She walked to the front door and let herself out.

Five minutes later he heard footsteps. "Your Highness?"

He turned in the direction of Francesca's voice and feasted his eyes on her beauty. When their gazes met, those fabulous brown eyes looked worried. Why? "I'm glad I caught you before you left for the day," he murmured.

"I was about to go home." She sounded a trifle breathless. "I'm afraid Daniel is away until tomorrow."

"I came to see *you* about the script for the video."

She blinked. "The script?"

He cocked his head. "I was hoping you would put down some of your thoughts and we could go over them while we grab a bite to eat."

"You mean this evening?"

He sensed she was nervous. "Do you still have another patient?"

"Yes," she responded too quickly, averting her eyes.

What was going on with her? "Do you mind if I wait?"

"I might be a while."

"That's no problem for me, Doctor. My mother says I'm the bane of her existence." He heard a slight chuckle. "How can I convince you that I won't bite?"

She let out a troubled sigh. "It's not that. I'm afraid that if you knew about my patient, it might make you sad."

"In what way?"

"I can see it's useless arguing with you. Come with me."

Relieved she wasn't fighting him anymore, he followed her down the hall to the examining room she used. No one was there, but he spied a crate on the floor with a dog inside. It whined and she spoke to it.

"I told you I'd be right back. We're going home."

Vincenzo hunkered down for a good look. A playful Bernese Mountain Dog, probably three months old, was in the last stages of puppyhood. The male reminded him so much of Karl at the same age, his heart felt a pang. Now he thought he understood Francesca's comment and was touched by her concern for his feelings.

He flicked her a glance. "Your new dog is made in Karl's image."

She nodded. "I knew it would remind you of him. Maybe too much. I couldn't resist this one the other day when he and his siblings came in for their shots. I'm crazy about the breed."

"That makes two of us. What's his name?"

"Artur."

"Well, Artur. What a lucky little tyke to have Dr. Linard for *your* owner."

"I hope he'll feel that way. I need to get him home."

"Let me help with any paraphernalia."

"You don't have to, but I guess I can't stop you."

"I'm glad you understand that, since it's clear my former dog and yours had a lot to do with this acquisition. I feel partway responsible." Nothing could have excited him more.

"Karl was special."

Amen.

"What do you need carried to your car?"

"That satchel on the chair. We'll leave through the back door."

When they reached the rear of the clinic, she removed her uniform and put it in the laundry bin. Vincenzo opened the self-locking door while she carried the crate. He would have done it for her, but knew the dog needed to trust her first. With the satchel in hand, he walked to the car and put it on the backseat next to Artur. The dog began whining.

He shut the door and went over to his car. They drove in tandem and within a few minutes reached her apartment complex. He carried her bags and the satchel up the stairs and into her living room. Her apartment felt cozy and comfortable.

"I'll take him outside and be right back." After putting a collar around the dog's neck and attaching a leash, she carried him out and down the stairs. The house training would go on and on. Vincenzo knew all about it.

Once back inside, she undid the leash and let the dog run around to explore while she set out water and food for him in the kitchen. More memories of early days with Karl filtered through his mind.

"What are you going to do with him during the days when you work?"

She followed the puppy around. His eyes followed her gorgeous figure. "Daniel said I could keep him with the other pets in the clinic's boarding kennel. They have their own backyard for a place to play. I think he'll love it. Of course, I'll have to take him out every few hours, but we'll be together."

"He'll be in doggie heaven knowing you're there too." Vincenzo unpacked the satchel and sacks. She'd been to a pet store and had bought a doggie bed and some fun toys.

He reached for the pack of jungle plush

pals and a rope to chew on. After getting on the floor, he rustled the rope around until her dog got excited and pounced on it. "Karl used to love to do this." For the next ten minutes the two of them laughed at Artur's antics as a tug-of-war ensued.

She got up from the floor. "I bought frozen pizza. Would you like some after I warm it up, Your Highness?"

"Sounds good." He continued to play with the dog while she fixed them a meal and called him over to the small dining room table. Artur whined for their food, but they knew better than to feed him.

"Sorry, buddy. Karl was a beggar too."

She laughed. "They all are, but I have a jerky dog treat for him." She unfastened a wrapper and made him reach for it. Her happy laugh and appealing personality were like an elixir to Vincenzo who never wanted to leave. But he was due at the palace at eight and they'd finished eating. He knew she had work to do with her new pet and got up from the table.

Artur ran over to him. Vincenzo gave him a quick rubdown. "Thank you for the pizza and salad, Dr. Linard. Now I must get going, but be warned—tomorrow evening after work, *I'll* be bringing our dinner to repay you. Maybe we can work on some of your thoughts to put in the video." His eyes found hers. "Have fun tonight. I envy both of you."

CHAPTER SIX

BOTH OF US?

Waves of heat swept through Francesca as she watched her dog follow him to the door. She locked up and had a full evening before going to bed. Artur lay in his new doggie bed in a corner of her bedroom. Like a child, he didn't want to go to sleep until she'd talked to him for a long time. Francesca couldn't sleep either. Not while her mind remembered every moment of the evening with the Prince.

To her amazement, she'd felt so comfortable with him she forgot he was Prince Vincenzo Baldasseri. He had sat on the floor laughing and playing with the dog. Everything had seemed to come naturally to him. The man was so easy to be around, and there couldn't be another one on earth as attractive.

Francesca had found that out after their day

of touring the biosphere where she'd discovered hidden depths to him. She'd had the time of her life. At this point it was more than a crush and it frightened her.

Prince Vincenzo wasn't a man you would ever let go. Her cousin had to be madly in love with him. Francesca could only imagine Valentina was in the depths of despair right now. Before long she expected to hear that his wedding to Valentina was back on.

She also needed to remember that his arranged engagement to her cousin had been broken recently. No doubt he was feeling the void in some way. Francesca had helped him with Karl and it was natural for him to be friendly with her. But not for one minute did she dare believe this bond between them would last.

If her cousin knew he'd spent this evening eating pizza with Francesca, a blood relative... The thought put the fear in her. Tomorrow evening she'd let him know once and for all that she couldn't be with him again except to do that one video. That was it!

After getting in bed later, she phoned her brother. "Rolf? I'm so glad you picked up!"

"Hey—what's wrong?"

She lay back against the pillow. "A lot has happened. Last week I had to put down Prince Vincenzo's dog. Karl was the sweetest thing and died peacefully."

"Your first patient and you had to put him to sleep," he commiserated. "I can only imagine how hard that was on you."

Rolf understood. In the next breath she told him about the conservation board meeting for the Biosphere Reserve and her trip there with the Prince. "He's asked me to help narrate the next video."

"Somehow that doesn't surprise me."

His comment caused her to sit up. "Why on earth would you say that?"

"I may be your brother, but I have eyes. You're even more beautiful than our cousin. Over the years my friends have commented on it. I'm not at all surprised the Prince is interested in you. But unlike them, he's not intimidated by you."

She trembled. "What are you saying?"

"The Prince is after you, Francesca. You're brilliant as well as gorgeous. That's hard on a lot of guys. When are you making this film?"

Her hand tightened on her cell. "Next month, but it's not a good idea."

"Why?"

"You *know* why." Heat swarmed into her cheeks. "I'm a Visconti and so was his fiancée."

"So? Didn't you just tell me that Dr. Zoller said it's over and the Prince has never been happier? If he'd loved her heart and soul, he wouldn't have broken with her. I can promise you that."

She clung to her cell while his logic sank in. "Even so, our cousin isn't just anyone. She's family, even though they don't recognize us. To spend any more time with the Prince she almost married would be…well, it would be—"

"Outrageous? Ludicrous?" he broke in with a laugh. "Come on. We're all humans first. Prince Vincenzo wants to get to know Dr. Linard, the vet. Admit you want it too! He has no idea that you're a Visconti in hiding. So go on being Dr. Linard and see where it leads."

"Rolf—don't joke about this."

"I know what's bothering you. You've finally met the man who turns you on."

"Rolf!" she snapped.

More laughter rolled out of him. "I knew it. Gina thinks he's a stud too, but I forgive her for that. I'm glad you called. This is the greatest news and I'll be waiting to hear the next episode of Dr. Linard's secret life in Scuol. It would make a great sequel to *All Creatures Great and Small*. Love you."

They disconnected.

After Francesca had been up part of the night with her dog, Friday morning came too soon. She took care of him and they left for the clinic. She had to hope Artur would learn to like the kennel. He whined his head off when she left him in the yard with the other dogs. But each time she appeared throughout the day to see to his needs, he'd settled down a little more.

Her working day involved two surgeries and the usual vaccinations and setting of limbs. She faced the end of the day with alternate feelings of excitement and dread over what was coming. They drove back to the apartment. Francesca had been going nonstop and felt it as she took care of her dog.

Every minute she listened for the Prince's approach. Until he arrived, she took advantage of the time to snap pictures of Artur with her phone to send to the family.

While she filled his water dish, he started

to bark. He hadn't done much of that yet. Someone had come to the door and knocked. Artur dashed toward it. Her heart almost palpitated out of her chest as she followed him.

Upon opening it, she came close to fainting. Vivid blue eyes beneath dark brows and wavy dark hair pierced hers. The Prince had come dressed in an open necked linen sport shirt and chinos, the epitome of an Adonis. He carried a sack of something that smelled delicious, but she couldn't think or concentrate.

The dog jumped around him making excited sounds. Artur smelled a friend as well as food. Francesca had to hold back her own excited feelings. "Come in, Your Highness."

He flashed her a smile, walked in and put the sack on the kitchen counter. Then he hunkered down to play with the dog. "I can see you're loving your new home, Artur. I brought you a present too." He pulled a canine party bone treat out of his pocket and unwrapped it. "These were Karl's favorites."

The dog grabbed it and ran off to chew on it.

Francesca stared down at him. "You're spoiling him."

He stood up. His eyes played over her features. "It's your fault." Those words and the way he said them made her legs go weak. "I hope you're hungry. I brought Chinese."

She swallowed hard. "You couldn't have picked anything I like more. If you want to freshen up, the bathroom is down the hall on the left."

"Thank you."

By the time he returned, she'd placed the food on the table. He'd also brought a bottle of wine which he poured into drinking glasses she'd provided.

"This is delicious," she said a few minutes later.

"I'm glad it tastes good to you." His eyes played over her. "What's your schedule tomorrow? I enjoyed our outing so much, I'd like to do it again. We'll take Artur to the mountains with us and discuss the script then."

She could hear Rolf's words. "He has no idea that you're a Visconti in hiding. So go on being Dr. Linard and see where it leads."

Francesca wanted to go with him so badly, she refused to listen to the warnings in her head. "If I come, you know we'll have a puppy with us and that means a lot of work."

He stared at her over his wineglass. "To be honest, I miss Karl and would love it more than you know." Francesca believed him. "I'll come by at eight thirty for you. Have a good night."

The second he left the apartment, Francesca sank down on the couch afraid over what she'd done. Should she have put the Prince off? What would happen if he found out who she *really* was? The dog sensed her distress and plopped himself in her lap. "Oh, Artur, have I made the biggest mistake of my life? What am I going to do?" When she finally put the dog down and went to bed, she sobbed into her pillow, tossing and turning all night.

Francesca's gorgeous image had been robbing Vincenzo of sleep. When Saturday morning came, he got up excited. Once showered and shaved, he pulled on a sport shirt and jeans. Before taking off, he wrote a message to be delivered to his mother that he had business this weekend. If an emergency cropped up, she should leave a message on his phone.

He drank his coffee and grabbed a roll to eat on his way out of the palace. Despite a warm August morning, he saw storm clouds gathering over the mountains in the distance. Nothing could dampen his spirits as he headed for Zernez.

After a stop at the deli, he drove to Francesca's apartment. She stood waiting at the bottom of the stairs with a bag and the crate next to her. He got out and helped her into his car. She looked beautiful dressed in jeans and soft pink pullover.

"It's your turn, Artur." After setting the crate in the backseat, he walked around and they took off. The dog barked when the thunder grew worse.

"Oh, dear," she murmured. "He's not used to it."

Vincenzo chuckled. "He's a mountain dog and will soon adapt. This weather couldn't be more perfect for him."

Like thieves stealing away in the night, they whizzed toward the mountains. He'd never known this kind of contentment. "Are you cold? Hot?"

"I'm perfect."

Yes, she is… "Tell me how your work is going overall."

"I love it. How lucky am I to do what I love for a living! What about your work?"

"When you're the only son of a prince, you're supposed to grow up doing what you're told to do. At first I wasn't that interested, but in time my views changed."

"How?"

"I saw the potential for expansion within the country and made new goals that would benefit the monarchy and some of my favorite causes. In that regard it turned out to be a good thing."

"The Biosphere Reserve is your case in point." She lowered her head, thinking of her father who'd done a great favor for her family. As a result of breaking with the Visconti side, her parents had allowed her and Rolf to lead their own lives.

"I'm afraid I wasn't as courageous in other areas." He made a turn that would lead them up the mountain to his chalet. "My father had dreams for me. Mother supported him in everything. The two houses of Baldasseri and Visconti decided to merge those dreams by arranging a marriage to Princess Valentina."

"How did *you* feel about that?" she asked in a quiet voice.

"I should explain something to you. From an early age I sensed my father, the younger brother, felt he was a disappointment to the Baldasseri family long before he married my mother. He suffered from terrible inferiority. I wanted to take away his pain because I loved him. The only way to do that was to be an obedient son. They raised me that I should enjoy dating, but never forget that when the time came, I would be marrying a princess."

"You obviously listened to them, which makes you a wonderful son."

"Not so wonderful, Francesca. After his death I realized how long I'd been lying to myself about what *I* wanted out of life."

A moan escaped her lips. "When did he die?"

"Soon after I was betrothed."

"I'm so sorry you lost him."

"It was hard. My mother is still grieving. They had a good marriage."

"So do my parents," Francesca admitted as a loud clap of thunder resounded, causing the dog to whimper.

Vincenzo reached back to knock on the crate. "We're almost there, buddy." The rain had started to splash down. He turned on the wipers.

"Your mother must be devastated that your marriage has been called off."

"I'm afraid so. One can only hope she will get over it. She cared for Valentina."

"What about your grandparents?"

"They don't say anything. Deep down I think Grandfather knows I'm not suffering over anything but the loss of Karl. I'm praying his kidneys hold out for a long time. I'll want his backing and my grandmother's when I decide to marry the woman I can't live without."

A noticeable pause ensued before she asked, "What about your sister?"

"Bella and I watch out for each other."

She nodded. "My brother and I are the same way."

"What are his plans?"

"He's in engineering right now and will marry his girlfriend, Gina, at Christmas. Is your sister betrothed?"

"No. She's taking her time. Mamma has ideas for her, but she's very particular. Between us she's searching for the perfect prince who we know doesn't exist."

Her laughter resounded. "I saw her picture on television while she was vacationing with Princess Constanza in Lausanne. What a beautiful girl! Actually, they both are.

I imagine they're besieged by any number of suitable princes."

"But none that either of them wants," he quipped.

He slowed down as the road curved around. The one-story chalet appeared nestled in the trees. "We're here, Francesca. I'm sure Artur can't wait to be let out. I'll go first and unlock the door. After you run in, I'll bring the dog and the groceries."

Francesca sat there in shock that the Prince had confided such private things to her. His ability to open up to her touched her to the depth of her soul.

He'd said they were coming to his little ski hideaway, but it was surrounded by pines and turned out to be an elegant Swiss mountain home with a vaulted ceiling, stone fireplace, two bedrooms with en suite bathrooms, a loft, dining area and a kitchen with every amenity. Hardwood floors were covered with area rugs. Francesca could live here forever in this paradise and wanted to explore. But Artur needed to go outside.

She attached his leash and walked him under a tree for some protection from the rain. Before coming with the Prince, she'd made a bed in the crate so her dog had a place to sleep near her. When she took him back inside, he'd put the crate near the fireplace with the door open. He'd also put out food and water bowls in the kitchen. Her dog darted for them. Artur had to be as wildly happy as she was to be here.

"Why don't you use the guest bedroom there on the right to freshen up while I make us a fire." A stack of wood stood next to the grate hearth.

She smiled. "When you mentioned a hide-away, I imagined a cot in a one-room cabin with a leaky roof and an outhouse in back."

Deep rich male laughter poured out of him. "My mother wouldn't have allowed it. Nothing was too good for her son. She makes certain it stays clean."

"Well, you can tell her for me, I'm *glad*." His chuckles followed her as she went in the bedroom with her bag. Before using the bathroom, she walked over to the window. The cloudburst had passed over. By afternoon they'd be able to go for a walk. She felt like she'd arrived in heaven.

A fire blazed as she went back to the living

room. She noticed that Artur was following him while he laid out a feast of pasta on the dining room table. "I can see my dog would rather live with you."

He lifted his dark head. "Then all I have to do is win *you* around and we'll all be happy."

Her breath caught at his remark. She wouldn't be here with him if she didn't want it far too much. "What can I do to help, Your Highness?"

A frown appeared. "The first thing I'd like you to do is call me Vincenzo."

Whoa.

"The 'Your Highness' business has gone on far too long."

She shivered in reaction.

"Why don't you get some wineglasses out of that cupboard and we'll eat. I don't know about you, but I'm famished."

"I am too."

In another minute they sat down at the table. He poured the wine. Everything about him appealed to her. When those brilliant blue eyes focused on her, she trembled inwardly from their fire. They began to eat.

"Deli food never tasted better," she commented in order to break the spell he'd cast on her.

"It beats my cooking," he quipped.

"And mine."

His gaze impaled her. "It has to be obvious to you by now that I want to get to know you better. I'm sorry if it feels like I've been hounding you. Forgive me. When you said you didn't feel right about doing the video, I should have accepted your decision as final and left you alone."

Francesca couldn't take this any longer. "I'm glad you didn't," she admitted in a shaky voice. "I really do want to participate in the project, but you're not just anyone. I've had a talk with my brother about you because… because you're a prince."

"And?" His eyes smiled. He was irresistible.

"He told me I was making a mountain out of a molehill."

More laughter poured out of him. "I've been called many things, but never that."

"Rolf believes in going with the flow."

"He sounds like my kind of man. I'm glad you listened to him, and your honesty disarms me. After I brought Karl into the clinic and met you, I talked with my sister where you're concerned."

She swallowed hard. "What advice did she have for *you*?"

"She didn't, because she knows that with my broken engagement behind me, I will make my own decisions about the rest of my life from here on out. *You* are one of them, yet I don't even know your first name."

Uh-oh. "It's Francesca."

"*The free one* in Latin. Beautiful. With your frank personality, it suits you more than you know."

She was starting to feel ill.

"I find I can't stay away from you, Francesca. Does that frighten you?"

Couldn't he hear her heart racing? "Yes."

"What can I do to make you feel more comfortable?"

Francesca looked away. "You can't."

He drank some wine, then put down his glass. "That's a word I don't recognize. I believe in my gut there *is* an us and I believe you know it too. Give me a specific I can live with, and I won't ever bother you again."

She drew in a quick breath. "If I tell you the reason, you're going to blame Daniel. I don't want to ruin your relationship with him. He thinks the world of you."

Vincenzo was totally intrigued. "And you. Otherwise he wouldn't have hired you or agreed for you to help with the video. What does Daniel have to do with your unwillingness to go out with me?"

"When I explain, I realize you're not going to want to have anything to do with me. But will you promise not to blame him?"

The depth of her anxiety spoke to him. "I swear it."

She clutched her hands beneath the table. "Since joining the clinic, I've gone by the name Dr. Linard. In truth, my birth name is... Francesca Giordano Visconti."

CHAPTER SEVEN

THE EARTH STOOD STILL for a second. "As in—"

"Princess Valentina Visconti," Francesca clarified for him.

Vincenzo's thoughts reeled. "How close a relationship?"

"Your former fiancée is my first cousin. Our Visconti fathers are estranged brothers."

The revelation stunned him. Both women were so different physically and emotionally, he would never have guessed that such a blood tie existed. He sucked in his breath. "Tell me more."

"My father, the former Prince Niccolo Visconti, fell in love with Greta Giordano, a commoner. Naturally it created a scandal because no Visconti had ever married a commoner before. Surely you know all about that history from Valentina. He made the decision to renounce his title and broke with the family. They moved to Bern where they married. He had business contacts there and started a packaging company."

He nodded. "When I first heard the story, I thought your father sounded like a man after my own heart."

"He's wonderful. In time, my brother Rolf and I were born and raised there. Neither of us has ever met the other side of the Visconti family. I've only seen pictures of Valentina on the news. There's been nothing between our families, but when I applied to Daniel's clinic which is in your territory, I had to be honest with him from the very start."

"I can see where this is heading. Go on. I want to hear everything."

She sat back in the chair. "During my interview, I had to explain the situation to him concerning the hostile history between the Baldasseri and Visconti families, and my relationship to Valentina. That's when he told me he was *your* vet."

Vincenzo smiled. "Quite a coincidence. We go back a long way and he knows a lot about my history."

"I couldn't believe he knew you so personally. I thought of course he'd turn me down for the position. Instead, he said he wanted to hire me. After he spoke to a government regulator, a waiver was signed so I could use any name I wanted. That way there would never be a connection. My brother and I came up with the Romansh name Linard. When you walked in the clinic with Karl the first time, my greatest fear was realized and I almost fainted."

"Meeting you turned out to be the greatest day of my life."

Her breath caught. "Don't say that—"

"Even if it's true?"

"But I've been living a lie. We can't see each other anymore, Vincenzo—" she cried. "You've just come out of an engagement to my cousin."

"A broken one that was arranged by both our families, not by *me* or Valentina."

Her head reared. "You're saying—"

"I'm saying exactly what you *know* I meant. Valentina and I were forced to meet only a few days before the engagement happened. Our families met at a regatta on Lake Garda where it was made official. Love had nothing to do with any of it.

"We were both guilted into making a commitment by our parents. We never slept together or came close. That was a commitment I made to my dying father. To Valentina's credit, she had the honesty to break it off while I've been trying to find a way for us to get out of it. Now we're both free and I've never been more relieved."

"Daniel told me how happy you were."

"He knows me very well. He also realizes that neither you or I could help that we've met each other, Francesca. You think I don't understand why you waited this long to tell me? I get it. Just remember that one day soon Valentina will be betrothed to someone else and none of this will matter anyway. In the meantime, it shouldn't stop us from enjoying a moment together here and there."

She shook her blond head. "It won't be here and there, Vincenzo, and you know it!" He watched the color flood into her cheeks. "I'm terrified to consider a relationship with you no matter how short-term."

"Why short-term?"

"Once word gets out about us and my true identity, it will bring grief to all the families, especially your mother. You said she cares for Valentina."

"That will fade with time, and we'll be discreet. Unless…" a dark brow lifted, "you've already had enough of my company."

"I wouldn't be here with you right now if that were the case."

"Grazie al cielo."

"Vincenzo, we need to use our heads." Staring straight into his eyes she said, "I don't want to see you after today."

"You're lying. I can tell by that nerve throbbing at the base of your tender throat."

She moaned. "Don't say anything else. You're not an ordinary man."

"But I am."

"No. You live in a different world, the same one my father left. You know I've enjoyed being with you to say goodbye to Karl. I feel honored that you would have allowed me to take care of him when I'm aware of your relationship with Daniel over the years. I'll make that video next month, but that's all there can be."

"I don't accept that. We feel an attraction that isn't going away."

"Even if you speak the truth, we can't act on it. Think about your mother."

He sat forward. "What's your greatest fear, Francesca?"

He heard her sharp intake of breath. "My father gave up one life to marry my mother and move away for good. I don't want my actions to create a new crisis for them. What's yours?"

Vincenzo finished off another helping of pasta and put his fork down. "That you're too concerned over my mother's attachment to Valentina to give us a chance."

"It's more than that. I'm her cousin. That fact alone will bring terrible pain to your mom."

"I've already accomplished that feat by not fighting for Valentina. I'll warn you now that I have no intention of this being our last day together, and I'm not talking about making the Biosphere Reserve video."

"But Vincenzo—" she blurted, "to go on seeing each other would be playing with fire."

"I'm more interested in the fire we feel when we're together," he countered. "It happened that first day. What we need is more time together, though no amount of trying to assuage our longing for each other will be enough for me."

Our longing? Vincenzo had just identified what was wrong with her. Francesca couldn't stay still and got up from the table. Artur followed her over to the fireplace. She hugged her arms to her chest and stared into the flames. Soon another pair of arms slid around her from behind.

Vincenzo pulled her against his tall, hard body and rubbed his cheek against hers. "I've been aching to do this since I discovered you at the clinic desk."

She'd been aching for it too. "Vincenzo," she moaned his name.

"Do you know at that moment my heart kicked against my chest? Who was this exquisite woman I wanted to take home with me? Lo and behold she turned out to be everything I ever wanted in a woman. What was more, she knew exactly what to do for my dog, enamoring him and me. I need to be closer to you, Francesca."

In the next instant he eased her around and his head descended. When his mouth covered hers, every sense sprang to life. The taste and feel of him thrilled her so much she found herself giving him kiss for hungry kiss.

Not until later would she realize how on fire she'd been for him and should have stopped what was happening. But she was in the moment right now and never wanted this ecstasy to end. Time passed as they clung, trying to get closer. Only Artur's barking could bring her out of her euphoria. She pulled away from Vincenzo in time to scoop up her dog.

"Did you feel ignored?" She kissed the top of his head and put him in his crate.

Vincenzo reached for her hand. "We're going to have to train him."

Her face felt hot as she looked up at him. His virile male beauty made her legs go weak. "My dog is smarter than I thought. He knew I was in trouble."

One corner of Vincenzo's compelling mouth lifted. "Your admission makes it easier for me to talk to you about us. Don't you dare say there is no us. At this juncture we both know better."

"I'd be a fool if I pretended otherwise." She moved to the couch and sat down. "But we need to be careful."

"So far I think we have been." He kissed her again and once more the world wheeled away to a place where only the two of them existed. By the time he relinquished her mouth and she came back to her senses, the sun had been out for a long time. She glanced down at the crate. "I'm afraid Artur gave up on us."

Their eyes met. "But you were right. He *is* a very intelligent dog. Let's find his leash and take him outside. We'll see if he looks for corncrakes the way Karl always did."

The three of them left the chalet and walked past the pines to a high meadow filled with blue gentians and yellow buttercups. Thrusting mountain tops formed the backdrop. They took a long hike, stopping every few steps to kiss because they couldn't stay away from each other. Artur scrambled around enchanted, mirroring Francesca's mood.

"The problem now is, I want to keep you here with me, Francesca. But I don't want you to think I'm trying to take advantage of you—therefore, I'm going to drive you home."

"You're asking me to leave paradise."

"Didn't you know that's the reason why?"

He kissed her fiercely. "Tomorrow's Sunday. I'll pick you up and we'll go on a picnic with Artur in the woods near the timber office. I know where you spend your working days. Now I want you to see where I spend mine. No one will be around but the night watchmen. That should be careful enough for you."

Vincenzo drove her back to her apartment. The only reason he could leave Francesca was because he'd be spending the day with her tomorrow. After saying good-night to the dog, he drove home. Intent on avoiding his mother who would ask too many questions, Vincenzo escaped to his suite in the other part of the palace.

Five minutes later he heard Bella's familiar knock on the door and he rushed to open it. "At last, you're home."

His beautiful, dark blond sister hugged him hard and they sat down together on the couch. "You don't need to say another word, brother dear. Mother is hopeless where you're concerned, but it's obvious that getting un-engaged to Valentina has done wonders for you. There's a light in your eyes I've never seen before. So now I want the whole truth.

What's really going on with you? I won't go away until you tell me."

Bella's return from vacation had been the medicine he'd needed and he unloaded on her. Those violet eyes of hers turned to a deeper tone as the revelation about Francesca's birth name and the story of her side of the Visconti family sank in.

He got up from the sofa and paced. "She's fighting me on this, Bella."

"Of course. That's because when word gets out, it'll create headlines across Europe. I can see them now, even though they won't be the truth—*Former Crown Prince Vincenzo Baldasseri of the royal family of San Vitano jilts Princess Valentina Visconti of Milano to take up with her estranged cousin Francesca Visconti, formerly of the House of Visconti.*"

Vincenzo grimaced. "The scenario is made for the media to plaster all over the world. Would you believe Francesca is worried about Mamma and her feelings for Valentina?"

"She sounds like a very nice person."

"Francesca is a lot more than that."

"She's right to be concerned. When our mother hears you've been seeing Valentina's cousin, she's going to explode."

"I'm not telling her yet. I need more time with Francesca first. Tomorrow I'm spending the day with her where we'll be alone."

"I can tell you've fallen hard, and there'll be no way she can resist you. I'm so happy for you. Considering she's a vet, her choice of dog tells you all you need to know about her feelings. Do you know when you showed me the photo of Artur on your phone, I thought I was looking at Karl. I miss him horribly."

"So do I," he murmured.

"You're going to have to find a creative way to convince her you're meant to be together."

"Thank heaven you understand. I want you to meet her and I'll arrange something. It'll have to be in private."

She got up from the couch. "Just let me know and I'll be there. Now I'll run to say good-night to the grandparents. Before I leave, I wondered if you've talked to Luca lately."

"Yes. He hasn't met anyone else yet."

A flushed Bella swept over to give him a kiss on the cheek. "Love you."

Early the next morning Vincenzo took off for Zernez. He stopped at a store for a picnic basket, then drove to the deli and filled it with food. Few clouds remained from yesterday's storm, increasing his joie de vivre.

When he pulled up to her apartment, she came hurrying down the stairs carrying the dog's crate and a bag. She wore a summery, short-sleeved print blouse and denims. The mold of her beautiful figure always took his breath.

He jumped out to put the dog and bag in the backseat. Before helping her in, he caught her to him and kissed her, unable to resist. Her flowery fragrance intoxicated him.

Artur made yapping sounds at being ignored, but they were both dying for each other. After Vincenzo started the engine, he reached back and slid a piece of jerky through the bars. "There you go, buddy."

Francesca smiled. "No wonder Karl loved you so much. I'm afraid maybe all this is a dream and I'm going to wake up to reality."

"We're both in the same dream, so if we wake up, we'll be together no matter where we are."

He drove them to the Baldasseri Timber Company outside Scuol. Located in the forest, the whole plant with its separate buildings could have taken up four city blocks. Beyond the structures lay a sea of trucks.

"Vincenzo—I had no idea of its massive size."

"This, along with the gold mine Rini heads, helps keep the Baldasseri family afloat. I thought you should see where I spend the bulk of my time."

He pulled up in front of the main entrance and turned off the engine. "Why don't I show you my office, then we'll drive to the area where Artur can get out and explore. We'll tie the dog's leash to this tree while we're inside."

"Perfect."

Several security men nodded to them as Vincenzo ushered her inside the foyer and led her down a hall past his assistant's office to his inner sanctum. The room contained one window behind his desk. There were a few chairs and a small table. What caught her gaze was the myriad of huge charts hanging on three immense walls and she let out a surprised gasp.

He slid his arms around her waist from behind. "This isn't like a normal office. I like to see what our business is doing. It's vital I keep my finger on all the areas where we plant and harvest trees. My working day consists of graphing the progress as the reports pour in. Each daily report reveals problems that need to be solved. This other chart displays my ideas for expansion. Little by little the business is growing."

"That's marvelous. I had no idea you were such a visual man. These charts are amazing! Another time and I want to study each one."

He turned her around, staring into her eyes. "I'm glad you said that because I want to take you somewhere totally private where I can study *you*."

Everything he said or did made her tremble with desire. "When did you start working here?"

"My father brought me here as a little boy. I learned all about the trees. He would test me. I had to name each kind and their best uses."

She grinned. "Let's see how good you are. What are they?"

His fantastic blue eyes ignited in challenge. "At four years of age I memorized them by their first letter in the alphabet—*A, B, F, L, M, O, P, S*."

She chuckled. "What do they stand for?"

"Ash, beech, fir, larch, maple, oak, pine and spruce. There are others, of course."

"Name one."

"The Swiss stone pine. Some call it the *Arolla*, known for its fragrance and ability to survive the winter."

"What tree is the most prolific?" she fired.

"The spruce, if we're talking the Engadin."

"It's apparent you were a brilliant student."

He kissed her mouth. "I knew after I met you that you're a woman with an exceptionally inquiring mind. It's just one of the reasons why I haven't been able to stay away from you."

Warmth spread through her body. She left his arms and walked over to one of the charts, astounded by the information. "So you work on these every day with your own set of hieroglyphs. Do I need a Rosetta stone to translate them?"

Vincenzo chuckled. "Probably something more complicated."

"That means your work would be difficult to decode. Can your assistant decipher them?"

"Most of the time."

"You're a genius! I'd like to learn."

"Come on, Dr. Linard. Let's leave the lab

work for another time." He walked over and put his arm around her shoulders. "Artur must be wondering why we've abandoned him."

Together they left the building. The dog heard them coming and started yapping before they put him back inside the car. Francesca put her hand back on the cage. "I know you were worried, Artur, but we didn't leave you very long. Now we're going to have fun."

She turned to Vincenzo who drove them into the forest. "Did you bring Karl to work a lot?"

"From time to time. To solve his loneliness on weekdays, I got up for work at five and left at three. Once home, I spent hours with him and took him with me most weekends. What's so perfect with your situation is that you can keep Artur in the kennel and check on him throughout the day. It's the ideal setup for him."

"I'm really lucky in that regard."

They reached a small clearing where he parked the car. "While you take care of the dog, I'll do the rest."

She carried the crate and a bag of doggie treats to a spot under the trees. After letting him out, she attached the long leash. "Come on, Artur. We'll go for a walk."

This glorious day in the mountains increased her feelings of joy to be out with the most wonderful man. How was it possible that she'd met anyone so perfect? Her ecstatic dog wanted to run everywhere and wore her out.

In the distance she watched Vincenzo spread a blanket near the crate. Next, he brought the picnic basket from the car. He thought of everything and always put her first.

Vincenzo grinned when Artur made a bee-line for him. He'd emptied bottled water into a bowl for the dog. She fastened the leash to the trunk of a tree. He carried the water over to Artur. Her dog drank and drank.

Vincenzo chuckled. "I hope you've built up a similar appetite, Francesca. Judging by the weight of this basket, I bought more than we can consume in one sitting. It was too late last night to ask the cook to pack us a meal."

She sank down on the blanket. "I have no doubts that she's like everyone who knows you, and would do anything for you."

"Does that include *you*?"

"I agreed to do that video narration for fear I'd never see you again."

"I came close to cardiac arrest until you said yes." He pulled her next to him and began kissing her. Slowly at first, until their passion grew to a whole new level. She felt him let her go with reluctance. "I think we'd better eat," he whispered, "or I'm going to devour you instead."

"When my brother accused me of finally meeting the man who appealed to me, I couldn't deny it."

"I already like him." He reached out to trace the line of her brow. "My sister said virtually the same thing about you."

She sat up. "Our siblings know us well."

They reached in the basket for the food they wanted and began eating. Vincenzo tossed the dog a piece of ham.

Francesca eyed him playfully. "I can see why Karl was so devoted to you. Artur already worships the ground you walk on."

"Flattery will get you everywhere." Vincenzo finished his second helping of everything before centering his gaze on her. "I'm curious about something. It's clear that you're not involved with another man right now, but have you been in love before?

"I can't imagine that you haven't been besieged with men wanting a relationship with you. No man could meet you without wanting to hide you away all to himself. You saw what happened at the board meeting."

Francesca had been listening with her heart and smiled. "I had several boyfriends at the university, but no one special. I take it you're talking about real commitment."

His eyes searched hers. "I had girlfriends, but I couldn't get serious because I knew I was destined to marry a princess. What happened to Valentina and me shouldn't have happened to two people who should be free to choose for themselves."

"I agree," she said in a shaky voice.

"This last year was the unhappiest of my life. What made it worse was meeting Dr. Linard. Clear as the sun coming out, she epitomized the woman I never imagined could come into my life. She was the woman I should have been able to get to know. She touched my mind and my heart. I love the way she thinks, how she feels."

Vincenzo...

"The day Valentina broke the engagement, you could have no comprehension of the joy that brought me. All my thoughts had been centered on this other woman from the first moment we met. We've known from the beginning that something magical has happened to us. Tell me I'm wrong."

"You're not mistaken." He was saying all the thrilling things she couldn't have imagined would come out of him.

"Don't tell me it's too soon, Francesca. I don't want to live a lie while I keep planning on how to get to know you better without anyone finding out."

She averted her eyes. "Nothing could be worse than trying to hide it. We couldn't anyway." It was her heart's secret desire to be with him. "But—"

"But nothing." He reached out to cup her hot cheeks in his hands. "I have a suggestion that could take away some of your fear."

"What do you mean?"

"I'd like to meet your parents. They're the ones you don't want to hurt. I'd like to be open with them and ask their permission for me to spend time with you."

She shook her head. "I don't think they'd give it."

"Maybe not, but it would be worth a try to find out."

Before she could concentrate, his mouth sought hers again. This marvelous man wanted to see her enough that he would brave meeting her parents.

"Francesca? If they're agreeable, we could arrange to drive to Bern next weekend. It's only a three-hour drive if *I'm* at the wheel." She couldn't hide her smile. "I could meet them and we'd talk. What do you think?"

"I don't know if this will work, Vincenzo."

"Let's put it this way. If your parents are against my seeing you, we have to find out right away. Could you try to get your parents on the phone now? If all goes well for a visit next weekend, then we'll make plans."

He was right. She couldn't fault his thinking. Francesca couldn't say no to him. "All right."

Having made up her mind, she took the big step to phone them. Vincenzo took care of the dog while she pulled the cell from her pocket. "Mom?"

"Francesca, darling. I was just thinking

about you. We love the pictures you sent of your dog. How's he adjusting to the kennel?"

"He likes being with the other dogs."

"What about your job? Are you happy?"

"You know I am. In fact, I'm happier than I've ever been. That's why I'm calling. I— I've met someone," she stammered. "It's a man who brought his sick dog into the clinic. We—"

A small cry of excitement came over the line, cutting her off. "Do you know how long your father and I have been waiting for that kind of news?"

"It's not *that* kind of news, Mom. I'm afraid it won't be what you want to hear."

"What do you mean?"

"We've only known each other for a short while. He wants your permission to take me out in public. We could drive to Bern next Saturday if it's convenient."

"Since when do you need permission?"

She closed her eyes. "His name is Prince Vincenzo Baldasseri of Scuol."

The flat-out truth had to come as a huge shock. Her mother paused before venturing, "As in your cousin's former fiancé."

She swallowed hard. "Yes. Their trumped-up

engagement was forced by their parents a year ago. It was never an affair of the heart for either of them. Now that it has been broken off, they both have been let out of prison. As you can imagine, he's more aware of the horrendous problems within the Visconti and Baldasseri families than anyone else alive, except you.

"In order for us to be seen together just to eat out at a restaurant, he realizes it could make the news and open up old wounds for you. But he refuses to hide in the shadows. I know he's right, even if it means we have to stop seeing each other. Because that's the kind of man he is, he won't go against your wishes. Neither will I."

More silence followed before her father joined in the conversation. "Francie?" It was the name he'd called her from childhood. "I've been listening to your conversation with your mom. I'm impressed by *this* Baldasseri. We'll be happy to meet him, but it will be better if we come to *your* apartment."

Message understood. His parents didn't need the attention. "You're right. Vincenzo is recognized everywhere."

"We'll come next Saturday and be there by lunch."

"I'll have it waiting for you. Artur will be ecstatic."

Her father chuckled. "I've loved all the names you've given your dogs, but this one kills me."

Tears filled her eyes over her parents' love and understanding. "Me too."

When she hung up, she turned to Vincenzo. "They're coming to my apartment next Saturday for lunch."

He folded her in his arms. "You have incredible parents." He kissed her hard. "With that call made, I have a plan for us. To make this real, I'm not going to try to be with you after work this next week. I'll go straight home from work each night and talk reason to my mother." Francesca's spirits sank. "But I want to see you every day for lunch."

Yes!

"When is your lunch break, Francesca?"

"There's no set time."

"Can you make one for us this next week?"

She nodded. "Let's say twelve thirty to one thirty."

He brushed his lips against hers. "I'm already wishing for tomorrow to come. Now I'd better get you home."

It was hard to leave. "We must drive your security men crazy driving all over the place."

"I try to keep them from being bored." He grasped her hand. "I'm relieved your parents are coming. All that's left is to gain their permission for us to be together, but I'm afraid we've put the proverbial cart before the horse."

"My father would laugh at that particular metaphor."

"I hope he's still laughing after we meet."

She prayed for that too. Her parents were marvelous, reasonable people, but this situation was unlike any story you could think up in your wildest imagination.

Once they reached the apartment, he helped her up the stairs with the crate and gave her another kiss. "I'll see you tomorrow. Miss me."

He had no idea.

CHAPTER EIGHT

WHEN VINCENZO REACHED the palace, he parked his car in a hidden area around the rear near a private entrance only he used. Filled with an excitement he'd never known, he raced up the back stairway to his suite so he wouldn't be detected.

Bella came to his room right after and shut the door. She leaned against it, putting a finger to her lips. They stared at each other. In a low voice she said, "Princess Valentina arrived this afternoon by helicopter and has been waiting for you. I tried to warn you."

His dark head reared. "Before I left yesterday, I sent Mother a message that I had business and would be gone for the weekend. Are you saying that Valentina just showed up?"

"Mother invited her and she's staying the

night because she doesn't want your engagement called off."

"But Valentina *did*. Something's not right, Bella."

"I agree. But you know Mamma. She's working on a plan that will get Valentina to change her mind and appease Stefano so the marriage goes forward. To make up for the fact that you're no longer the Crown Prince, she's going to give you and Valentina her royal Sardinian inheritance from the sheep-farming industry. It should work."

"That inheritance still doesn't touch our timber assets and won't satisfy Stefano. Valentina won't buy it either." In record time he packed a bag. "Does she have any idea I'm here?"

"No."

"Did anyone see you just now?"

"I passed one of the maids in the hall."

"We can't worry about that now." Vincenzo shut the lid. "I'm leaving and won't be back until after work tomorrow." He rushed toward her and gave her a kiss on the cheek. "You're an angel to run interference. I'll fill you in later tonight. Expect a phone call after you go to bed."

Before another second passed, he slipped out of the palace and down the private stairway. Only his bodyguards trailing him would know where he was headed. Their unquestioned loyalty would keep his secret safe. He couldn't say as much for the staff.

Once he arrived at the chalet, he got ready for bed and phoned Bella. After telling her about his plans to meet Francesca's parents next weekend, his sister sounded overjoyed. "You can count on me to help you in any way I can." They hung up and he lay back down. Next weekend couldn't come soon enough for him to meet her parents. In the meantime, he'd be able to see her throughout the week.

At twelve thirty on Monday, he watched Francesca leave through the back door of the clinic and hurry to his car. His pulse always raced when he laid eyes on her.

Vincenzo reached across the seat to open the door for her and drove them to the park where they had privacy. He kissed her soundly before they ate the deli food he'd picked up.

When they'd finished, he said, "Francesca? I have something to tell you. Though I'd rather hold back from saying anything because I don't want to ruin our lunch, this can't wait and has to be said. I would never keep anything from you."

She turned to him. "You sound so serious."

"I wish it weren't."

"You're starting to scare me."

"I don't mean to do that. Last night I returned to the palace to grab some sleep. I entered through a doorway rarely used so no one would see me. To my shock, Bella followed me into my bedroom. She'd tried to reach me by phone, but I didn't take any calls. She told me Valentina had flown to the palace by helicopter earlier in the day and was staying overnight."

"What?"

He nodded. "It seems my mother invited her so the three of us could talk about a reconciliation."

"That means Valentina wants you back."

"I don't think so since she's the one who called off our engagement. There's some mystery here I don't understand, but I'm going to get to the bottom of it."

"Your mother wants you to marry Valentina."

He shook his head. "There's more to it than that. I told Bella I wasn't staying and left the palace the same way I came in. Last night I returned to the chalet to sleep. When I talked to my sister at midnight, she said she didn't believe anyone knew I'd even been there. She texted me this morning after Valentina left in the helicopter to let me know the coast was clear."

"What are you going to do? Are your grandparents applying pressure too?"

"No, but they try to support my mother now that my father is no longer with us."

"Your poor mother wants you to be happy."

He grasped her hand. "I've never been happier in my life. One day soon she'll understand."

"I don't know, Vincenzo. She's lost your father and now all her dreams have been shattered."

"But they aren't *my* dreams." He leaned over to kiss her once more. "Let me finish. The simple truth is, I've fallen in love with you, deeply in love. You may say it's too soon for you to know what's in your heart. Maybe knowing how I feel, you would prefer that we don't see each other again. You can cancel the plans with your parents if that's your wish. But I'm well acquainted with my feelings and can't hold back what matters to me more than anything else in the world. I love you."

He waited until her brown eyes looked into his. She breathed deeply. "Do you think I would have spent time with you from the beginning if I didn't have feelings *I* can't deny? Your honesty has forced me to reveal what's in my soul. I love you too, Vincenzo, more than I ever thought possible. I'm so in love I'm almost sick over it."

"*Francesca*—you're the woman I'll adore forever." He pulled her against him and kissed the mouth he could never get enough of. "I know this is the wrong place to pour out my heart, but I can't help it. More than ever I need to meet your parents, to know if there's hope for a future. Speaking hypothetically, how would you feel about being married to a man who runs a timber company?"

She wrapped her arms around his neck. "You already know the answer to that. I loved every minute with you yesterday, and can't wait to learn more. The real question is, how would you feel about having a vet for a wife? I'm hardly the choice for a prince."

He smoothed the hair off her forehead. "The moment I met you, thoughts of Daniel helping me with Karl left my mind. You filled my every need and Karl loved you. I knew at once that no other woman could ever satisfy me while I lived on this earth."

"*Vincenzo*... It happened that way for me too," she confessed.

"The next question is, are you happy working for Daniel?"

"Totally."

"Then our only problem would be where we live."

Her heart pounded harder. "The palace is your home."

"Do you know I lived more than four years in a private dwelling in Scuol?"

"I can understand that."

He flashed her that compelling smile. "Naturally I paid visits home, but I liked my bachelor life with Karl, and only went back to the palace to live after my father died. My mother and grandparents needed me." He cocked his dark head. "Do you love your apartment?"

"Very much."

"I like it there too. It already feels like my home away from home. Were we to marry—I'm speaking hypothetically—how would you feel if I moved in there with you where you'd be close to your work?"

She bit her lip. "But Vincenzo, you're a—"

"Don't say it." He put a finger to her lips. "Forget I'm a prince."

"I do, most of the time."

"That's good. What's even better, your apartment is only a twelve-minute drive to my work. I've timed it." She chuckled. "On weekends we could stay at the chalet, or at the palace. Whatever we feel like."

"But your family will want you to live there with them all the time."

"You're wrong. They've had no future expectations about that. If Rini hadn't recovered his memory, Valentina and I would have been forced to live at the palace in San Vitano after the marriage. My great-uncle King Leonardo wanted me near him."

She shook her head. "So much has changed."

"Since meeting you, I feel reborn." He pulled her closer. "*Ti amo*, Francesca."

"*Ti amo*, Vincenzo. That much isn't hypothetical."

Their hunger knew no boundaries. No kiss was long enough or deep enough to satisfy them, but this couldn't go on. "I need to get you back to the clinic."

"I know." She eased out of his arms and sat over on her side of the car.

He started the engine and they left the park. Her admission of love had transformed his world. "Our talk has settled many questions that have made me happy beyond belief. My biggest worry is that your parents will decide they don't want me pursuing you. If that happens—"

"Don't think that way," she broke in. "They fought against the odds to find their happiness. I have to believe they'll grant us the same chance. My worry is that your mother won't be able to accept me."

"I'm working on it." He started the car and drove them the short distance to the clinic. It was a wrench to have to leave her arms. An hour wasn't enough time.

When he parked, she turned to him. "Come to my apartment tomorrow at twelve thirty and we'll eat there. Tonight I'll fix our lunch and have it ready."

"Have I told you before that I love the way your mind works, *bellissima*? Much as I want to, I don't dare kiss you again."

She leaned over and kissed his lips gently. "Until tomorrow."

To his relief, the rest of his work week had never been busier. Their lunch dates kept him sane, but nothing stopped him from counting the hours to see her. Each night he called to let her know of his love and what was going on.

"Is there any more news about Valentina?"

"Only that my mother is worried about her. The breakup has caused her to be distraught."

"But that makes no sense."

"No, it doesn't. My mother is begging me to make things right. She's positive that if I get back with Valentina, she'll be herself again. Mamma is in denial. I don't know what it's going to take to make her see reason, but she'll have to in time."

"I don't know."

"I *do*." He and his mother had reached an impasse. Vincenzo was living for the meeting with Francesca's parents. Everything hinged on their approval. If it was given, life was going to go in a new direction no matter what.

At ten to ten on Saturday morning, Vincenzo knocked on Francesca's apartment door. He held the sack of groceries with the ingredients they'd decided on for this important meal. Adrenaline surged through his body as he anticipated what this day would mean for the two of them.

Artur kept barking. When she opened the door, he put down the sack and reached for her. "You look sensational and smell divine. I like your outfit," he murmured, eyeing the dark skinny denims and attractive hoodie.

The soft, pale green set off her coloring. Her brown eyes looked alive as they studied his blue pullover and cargo pants. The dog kept running around his feet, finally breaking the trance that held them both.

"Artur—" she called to him so Vincenzo could walk inside with the sack. He lowered it on the kitchen counter, then hunkered down to play with the dog. He'd missed him like crazy. The building attachment warmed his heart. But there was another attachment so strong, it propelled him to Francesca's side. She'd started emptying the sack.

He slid his arms around her and pulled her against him. "Good morning, Dr. Linard. Our daily lunch hours weren't nearly enough to satisfy me." In the next breath he covered her mouth with his own. Like flame to kindling they lost track of time pouring out their hungry need for each other. The taste of her, the way she felt in his arms filled his heart and drove every other thought from his mind.

"*Ti adoro*, Francesca," he cried against her lips.

"*Ti amo anch'io*," she answered. Her confession of love thrilled him in every fiber of his being. They clung until she had the presence of mind to ease out of his arms. "If I don't get started on this lunch, there won't be one."

They'd planned cheese fondue with French bread and Riesling wine. Vincenzo got busy helping her. While he set the table he said, "This is the most important meeting of the century. I want your parents' blessing more than anything I've ever wanted in my life."

She finished grating the cheese. "So do I. But what if they don't give it?"

"Do you honestly think they won't?"

"I—I don't know…" Her voice faltered. "This is one situation none of us could have imagined."

He put the wineglasses on the table. "In that

case, how do you feel about a quick elopement? That would solve everything. We'd be total outcasts and start a new life where we're unknown. You could set up a vet practice and I would help you."

A smile broke out on her beautiful face. "I'd love it. But you're teasing of course."

This woman had been made for him. "I've never been more serious, Francesca."

"I know you are. That's why what you've said is so scary." Her comment coincided with the sound of footsteps outside the door, followed by a familiar knock. Artur barked.

Vincenzo's gaze flew to hers. "This is it."

"I'll let them in." She washed her hands and hurried over to let her parents inside.

As Vincenzo put bread and fondue forks on the table, he watched the loving affection the three of them had for each other. Francesca resembled both parents. She'd inherited her mother's attractive looks and her father's smile.

"Mom? Dad? I'd like you to meet Prince Vincenzo Baldasseri."

"Your Highness," they said in unison.

Vincenzo stepped forward to shake their hands. "Call me Vince."

"If you'll call me Niccolo."

Vincenzo had already been prepared to like him. The Visconti brothers shared a resemblance in their dark coloring and firm body builds. But Francesca's father had softer features and laugh lines not apparent in Stefano Visconti.

Francesca hugged her mother's waist. "Vincenzo, this is my mother, Greta."

"Signora Visconti. I've been waiting anxiously for this day."

"I'm Greta, and I've been eager to meet you too, Prince Vincenzo."

He was charmed by her. "Please let me be Vince to the two of you. Francesca is definitely your daughter. Among other lovely traits, she has your blond hair and warm brown eyes."

"They trapped me the first time we met," her father volunteered.

Yup. Vincenzo knew the feeling.

"You two have had a long drive," Francesca broke in. "Why don't you freshen up in the guest bedroom and bathroom down the hall while I put the dog in his crate. Otherwise, he won't leave us alone. Then we'll enjoy some fondue while we talk."

* * *

Francesca's parents were so wonderful and made Vincenzo feel so comfortable, she could have cried out for joy. The four of them ate fondue and drank their wine while she told them how Karl had brought her and Vincenzo together.

"After I put him down, we drove to the mountains where he used to play. I found myself wanting a dog just like him and fell in love with Artur. One thing led to another, and here we are." She darted Vincenzo a glance. "The dog is already attached to him."

Vincenzo sat back in the chair. "As the two of you are aware, I've become attached to your daughter. The bizarre coincidence that she's a Visconti couldn't have shocked me more. She was Dr. Linard to me."

Her mother nodded. "No one could question the innocent circumstances under which you met."

"The truth is, from the moment she greeted me, the instant attraction I felt for her was like nothing I've ever experienced in life and has only grown stronger. What made it so shocking was that I was still engaged to Valentina."

Her father shook his head. "When did your engagement come to an end?"

"A few days after I took Karl to the clinic. Later I received a call from my cousin Rinieri. He told me he'd recovered from his amnesia and was relieving me of the duty of Crown Prince. I'd never been so happy with the news that I wouldn't have to be King one day. A few days later Valentina broke our engagement. It has upset my mother."

"Of course. I've been through a traumatic experience in my own family," her father revealed. "When they couldn't be happy for me and Greta, we left Milano for good."

"Francesca told me." Vincenzo leaned forward. "I explained to her that my engagement to Valentina had been arranged by both families. The truth is, I was never in love with her. By the time I'd heard from Rini, I'd already met Francesca and understood what it meant to find that perfect someone you knew could fill your whole life. That's why I asked her if I could meet with you. I'd like your blessing to go on seeing her."

She felt her father's eyes on her. "Do you feel the same way?"

"Yes. It's why I called you."

"Even knowing all the repercussions that are going to happen?" This from her mother.

"Yes. But I'm afraid this could hurt the two of you, which is the last thing we want."

Her father reached for her mother's hand. "We've already been through our Gethsemane. Don't worry about us."

Vincenzo finished his wine. "I'm afraid there already is a problem that might influence how you feel about Francesca and me."

"Go on," her father prodded him.

"My sister told me that my mother invited Valentina to stay at the palace a week ago to try and get the two of us back together. I was away spending time with your daughter and didn't know anything about it.

"My mother wants to affect a reconciliation of which I want no part. I knew I had to meet with the two of you and let you know my intentions before I took Francesca to meet my mother and grandparents. The sooner they understand the situation, the better. Today, if it were possible, but that's asking a lot. Maybe too much."

A smile lit up her father's face and eyes. "Nonsense, Vince. I admire you for doing the honorable thing and putting Francesca first.

You're wise to do this right away. You have our backing."

"Dad—" Francesca cried for joy.

Vincenzo got to his feet. "That means more to me than you will ever know."

Her mother grabbed Francesca's hand. "I couldn't be happier for both of you, and I have an idea. If you two want to leave for the palace now to state your case, your father and I will tend Artur and stay the night."

Francesca looked at Vincenzo whose indigo blue eyes blazed with light. His were asking if she wanted to accept her parents' offer. Their approval meant everything. "Vincenzo? If we go, you'll need to inform your mother that we're coming."

"I'll do it now."

"Use my bedroom. While you do that, I'll take out the dog."

"And *I* will do the dishes," her mother piped up.

Her father got up first. "I'll clear the table."

Out of the corner of her eye she saw Vincenzo shake her father's hand. But her parent had other ideas and gave him a hug. Nothing could have thrilled her more. She put the leash on the dog and took him out. "I promise you're going to love my parents, Artur."

A half hour later Francesca had changed to a light blue summer suit and they headed for Scuol. "You look fantastic." Vincenzo grasped her hand and never let it go during the short trip. "Meeting your parents has explained you as nothing else ever could. They're beyond remarkable."

"I'm glad you like them. They obviously approve of you."

"My prayers have been answered, but the meeting with my family won't resemble what just happened with your parents."

"I'll be fine because I know my folks are behind us. Does your family know what this is all about?"

"No. I simply told my mother I needed to meet with the three of them right away and that I was bringing someone important with me."

"Any more word of Valentina?"

"No. According to Bella there have been phone calls."

"Dare I ask about that?"

"I didn't give Mamma a chance to talk, only that I would be home shortly."

After his mother thought she could reconcile her son and Valentina, she would go into shock when she met Francesca. So deep were her thoughts, she didn't realize they'd arrived at the palace until he'd parked his car in the rear and shut off the engine.

"Before we go in, I need this." He leaned over and kissed her with a thoroughness that left them both shaken.

"Just follow my lead." He got out of the car and walked around to help her. "We'll go up the back stairway to the drawing room on the second floor. My grandfather will be in his wheelchair."

He squeezed her waist as they walked past several guards and climbed the stairs of the elegant palace. When they reached the drawing room, he led her to his mother, then his grandparents where they were introduced to her. She didn't see his sister.

From his grandfather, who had lost most of his hair, she could tell from his long legs he was a tall man. Through the bone structure of his attractive features, Vincenzo got the fabulous looks of his Baldasseri genes. She also saw facial traits from his striking mother with her auburn hair. His grandmother was a lovely, older white-haired woman.

Vincenzo guided her to a love seat where they sat down. He clung to her hand. "Thank you for being willing to meet with me today because I have an announcement to make." All eyes focused on him with guarded anxiety.

"In the last month, a number of changes have happened in my life that have transformed me. First came the news that I'm no longer the Crown Prince of San Vitano. Following that came my broken engagement. Thirdly, and the most important one, I met the woman with whom I've fallen in love."

Gasps came out of the women. Francesca noticed his grandfather exhibited no reaction.

"I introduced her to you under her professional name Dr. Francesca Linard, a vet from the Zoller Veterinary Clinic in Zernez. She was the one who treated Karl and put him to sleep. What you don't know is that I soon learned her birth name is Francesca Giordano Visconti, daughter of Greta and Niccolo Visconti."

Vincenzo's mother got to her feet. *"Visconti?"*

Francesca's heart began to palpitate hard.

"That's right, Mamma. As I'm sure Valentina would have told you, there was a falling out in the Visconti household years ago. Prince Niccolo married a commoner and they moved to Bern, Switzerland. He rescinded his title and severed all ties with the royal House of Visconti. Later on, Francesca and her brother Rolf were born. She and Valentina are first cousins, but they've never met."

"You mean to tell me you're involved with Valentina's cousin? The woman you were engaged to for the last year?" His mother's shock and pain pierced Francesca's heart.

Vincenzo's blue eyes fell on Francesca. "For now and always."

Oh, Vincenzo... I love you so much.

"I haven't officially proposed yet, or given her a ring, Mamma. Only today did I meet her mother and father and ask their permission to get to know her better. Now that I have it, I've come to my family to ask for yours."

His grandfather shook his head. "You can't see her again, Vincenzo."

Francesca thought she'd been ready for his reaction, but it still hurt like a stab in the heart.

"I'm sorry you feel that way, Nonno, but my heart has dictated otherwise."

"There's another reason besides your heart that forbids it. This is a discussion you must have with your mother." He started to wheel himself out of the room. His wife got up and helped him. When they'd left the drawing room, his mother sat back down with her hands clasped.

"What other reason was Nonno talking about, Mamma?"

"It would be better if you and I were alone, my son."

Vincenzo squeezed the hand he'd been holding. "Francesca and I are together in everything."

His mother sat straighter. "Very well. Valentina flew to the palace a week ago and stayed overnight."

"Bella told me."

"Bella doesn't know everything."

"Then *you* tell me."

"Valentina is pregnant with your child. She just had it verified with her doctor. That's why she flew here, to tell you in person. More than ever it's imperative the two of you arrange to be married as soon as possible."

"I'm afraid it won't be possible. I was never in love with her and it's not my child. We never slept together."

Vincenzo had told her as much. The news had meant everything to Francesca. She held her breath waiting for his mother's response.

"Valentina wouldn't lie to me."

In the next instance Vincenzo got to his feet. "*I've* never lied to you. How far along is she?"

His mother lowered her head. "She said two months."

"Did you tell you all this in front of my grandparents?"

"Of course."

He shifted his weight. "Since I brought Francesca to the palace to meet my family, we'll discuss Valentina's dilemma later. Under the circumstances, I'll drive her back to Zernez. When I return later, I'll say goodnight to you and the grandparents."

Francesca groaned to see his mother so devastated. She didn't know that her son had been telling the truth.

CHAPTER NINE

VINCENZO REACHED FOR Francesca's hand and
ushered her out of the drawing room. They
didn't speak going down the stairs and out the
doors of the palace. Before he helped her in
the car, he pulled her against him and rocked
her in his arms. "I'm so sorry for what happened. This wasn't the way this day was supposed to end."

She threw her arms around his neck, aching over the unexpected news that had complicated his life and hers. "Don't worry about
me. It's your mother's disappointment I'm
feeling."

"Thank you for believing me, and being so
sweet about my mother. Unfortunately Valentina couldn't have done anything to raise
Mamma's hopes more than to tell her she
was pregnant. If it's true, then this situation

is proof that her arranged engagement didn't work. But if she isn't pregnant, then this is a ruse perpetrated by Stefano to get what he wants."

"Either way it's tragic, Vincenzo." She was heartsick.

He nodded. "Valentina pretended to be happy with our betrothal in front of the family, but this announcement is about to turn her life into a nightmare." He gave Francesca a swift kiss. "Come on. Let's get you home."

Back in the car, they headed for Zernez. "What are you going to do, Vincenzo?"

"I'm flying to Milano in the morning and confront Valentina. I don't know if she's pregnant or not. Before I met her, I heard she liked to party and had various boyfriends. Though she denied she was involved with anyone when we met, I didn't believe it. If she's pregnant, there is someone else of course."

"But not the man her family had picked out for her," Francesca murmured.

"She could be pregnant and two months along. But thanks to modern medicine, a DNA test can be done at nine weeks to prove paternity without injuring her or the baby.

I'll go to her doctor with her and we'll soon learn the truth."

Francesca shivered. "What if she refuses?"

"In that case I'll go to her father and insist. The sooner she gets the test that proves I'm not responsible, the sooner she can sort out her life."

"Do you think her father will cooperate?"

"I doubt it. He's a very difficult man." Vincenzo turned his head to glance at her. "First I'll attempt to reason with Valentina."

"In her state, I don't know if that's possible."

"Maybe not," he said, making a turn near her apartment. "Why don't we discuss it with your parents? No one knows Valentina's father better than your own father. Perhaps he can shed some words of wisdom."

"My parents won't welcome this news."

"Would you rather I didn't tell them what happened?"

She shook her head. "The truth has to come out."

Vincenzo parked the car and turned, pulling her against him. "Don't you know I'd give anything to spare you all this?"

"I feel the same way about you. We'll get through it."

"Yes, we will, my love." He kissed her with exquisite tenderness before they went up to the apartment. Before they reached the door, she could hear Artur barking.

"Now I know I'm home," she whispered against his lips before the door opened.

"Whoops." Her mother's small cry brought a smile to Francesca. "Come on in, you two."

They moved inside while the dog jumped up and down around them. Francesca picked him up and sat down on the couch, holding him on her lap.

Vincenzo planted himself next to her and put his arm around her shoulders.

Her mum and dad sat on the stools at the island in the kitchen drinking coffee. "Welcome back. You're home earlier than we expected, Francie."

"We had an unexpected evening, Dad."

"What happened?"

Vincenzo sat forward with his hands clasped between his knees. "After introducing Francesca to my grandparents and mother, she greeted us with news we hadn't anticipated." In the next breath he explained that Valentina had flown to the palace and told the family she was pregnant with Vincenzo's child. "Both families want the marriage to take place as soon as possible."

The stunned look on her parents' faces brought him to his feet. "I told them the baby wasn't mine. I'm flying to Milano Monday morning to confront Valentina and her parents. My mother says she's two months along. Thanks to modern medicine, a test can be done. Then the truth of paternity will be known for all to see."

Francesca's mom slid off the stool. "I promise that her family will fight you before you can demand she get that test."

At this point Francesca got up from the couch and lowered the dog to the floor. "We're ready. Do you have any advice that could help?"

She watched her father walk over to Vincenzo with a gleam in his eyes. "Indeed, I do. I want you to inform the brother I haven't seen for years that you and my daughter are involved. Tell him *I* insist on the DNA test."

"Thank you, Niccolo. Good night, Greta." The two men shook hands. "I need to leave now. Francesca? Will you come out to the car with me?"

She followed him outside. He had no words and simply crushed her in his arms. "I'll phone you tomorrow. *Sogni d'oro.*"

She would need sweet dreams.

Monday morning the helicopter landed behind the Visconti palazzo. Vincenzo told the pilot to stay put. He wouldn't be here long.

Valentina, dressed in a pink suit and pearls, came running toward him with her dark hair flouncing about her shoulders. She was taller than Francesca. He could find nothing about her that reminded him of the woman he loved. She greeted him with a kiss on his cheek. "Thank you for coming so quickly."

He took an extra breath. "The second my family gave me your news, you *knew* it would bring me as soon as I could make plans."

"It's so good to see you, Vincenzo. Won't you kiss me? Really kiss me." Her eyes beseeched him. Why? For whose benefit?

"We're no longer engaged, Valentina." He reached for her hand. "Come on. Let's go for a walk where we can talk in private. This will only take a few minutes since I have to fly back to my office ASAP."

She held back. "You can't leave! We have so much to plan. The family has arranged a special lunch for us in the small dining room upstairs. Vincenzo—" she protested in exasperation as he pulled her toward the rose garden to the east.

When he came to a bench, he put his hands on her shoulders and set her down. "I don't know whether it's your family or you who has decided that our former engagement is back on, but I'll let you know now. It will never happen."

"Even knowing I'm pregnant?"

"It's not my child, Valentina."

A look of terror filled her eyes. "No one else knows that."

Ah. She *was* pregnant!

That was all he'd needed to hear. He sat down next to her. "The truth will come out when you go to the doctor for a DNA test. Mother says you're two months along. In another few days you'll be able to have it done and name the father."

"I'll do no such thing." She jumped to her feet. "It's a dangerous procedure."

"Not true. In today's world it's safe for you and the baby."

"I absolutely refuse. You and I are going to get married." She'd dug in her heels, confirming his suspicions that her agenda had to do with her father.

Vincenzo got to his feet. "A year ago we entered into an arranged engagement. A few weeks ago, you called it off. Neither of us was in love. Proof of it is the baby you're carrying. I don't want to be unkind, but you need to marry the father of your child."

"I can't." He heard pain.

"That's between the two of you. He deserves to know you're expecting his baby. There's nothing else to discuss and I have to leave."

She cocked her head, gazing at him through narrowed lids. "I have no intention of getting that test. You and I *will* be married soon."

"Says your father? Afraid not, Valentina."

"Don't be too sure."

Vincenzo felt sorry for her, but he'd had enough. *"Arrivederci, Principessa."*

He wheeled around and walked in swift strides to the helicopter. Once strapped in the copilot's seat, he watched Valentina run toward the palazzo before she was out of sight. This morning's short visit was the last one he would ever make to the Visconti palazzo.

Once he reached the timber office, he phoned his mother and told her to expect him and Francesca that evening. Since his visit with Valentina, he had news. The three of them needed to talk.

At ten to three he was going over the latest reports at work when his assistant Fadri buzzed him. "You have a visitor, Your Highness. He doesn't have an appointment."

"Who is it?"

"Prince Stefano Visconti of Milano."

Vincenzo had wondered how long it would take Valentina's father to intervene. He'd never cared for Stefano, but at the time of the engagement, Vincenzo had been prepared to try to get along with him. The fact that he'd come in person to surprise him rather than phone him first indicated the depth of his desperation.

"Show him in, Fadri."

In a minute Valentina's father stormed in and shut the door. Vincenzo stood up. "Stefano? Come all the way in and sit down. I'll have coffee brought in for you."

"I won't be here long enough," came the wintry response. "You can't duck your responsibilities, Vincenzo. You may no longer be the Crown Prince, but we'll overlook that setback and arrange the wedding for two weeks from today."

Stefano didn't even try to hide the reason for the engagement being called off.

"I hope you mean with the man who impregnated your daughter. I wish her and your family the very best."

Anger brought red patches to the other man's cheeks. "We both know the name of that man."

"I'm afraid *I* don't. But as I told Valentina—whom I've learned is two months along—she can have a test done to prove paternity. That should still give you time to plan a wedding for her and the man she loves."

Stefano's body stiffened. "Your insolence is unconscionable. I've already given the news to the media about the wedding date for you and Valentina. By tomorrow morning it will be all over Europe."

Vincenzo sat back in his chair. "Then the Visconti family will have another sensational story on its hands you'll have to live down."

"Another?" he asked in an acid tone.

"Have you forgotten the incident with your brother? If you recall, he left Milano and got married. You have a niece, Francesca Giordano Visconti, who happens to be Valentina's first cousin, albeit they've never met. Francesca and I met at the veterinary clinic in Zernez where she introduced herself as Dr. Linard to avoid name recognition. We've fallen in love and are seeing each other exclusively."

"I believe you've lost your mind."

"No. Talk to the owner. Dr. Zoller will verify what I've just told you. The news about me and Francesca will give the media endless joy as they exploit the ongoing saga from the illustrious Houses of Visconti and Baldasseri."

Stefano's eyes darkened in fury. "What piece of fiction is this?" he hissed.

"Ask my mother. She knows all about it. If that doesn't satisfy you, ask your brother and his wife. They'll answer any of your questions."

"I don't believe one word coming out of your mouth."

"You will if you give a false story to the newspapers about your daughter and me. It will cause another media frenzy that will rebound on you. If I were in your place, I'd go home and insist Valentina get that test done before you announce your daughter's intended marriage to the wrong man."

"Your lies won't get you out of this. Valentina foolishly broke the engagement because you neglected her, but she has since regretted that action due to her pregnancy."

"You mean due to the timber shares you've been praying to get your hands on no matter the cost? I never neglected her and I have my pilot's logs to prove I flew to Milano for every single date made. Don't keep trying to turn this around, Stefano."

He wheeled around and opened the door. Before leaving, he yelled, "You're lying!"

"Then I suggest you phone Niccolo. What's it been? Close to thirty years without contact? He'll put you straight before it's too late."

"It's over for you! I'll take you to court and sue you for breach of contract to marry."

"I don't think so. Valentina broke our engagement."

"You broke her heart," Stefano raged.

Vincenzo shook his head. "I think you've been doing a good job of that yourself."

Stefano shook his fist at him. "You'll be sorry when I get you in court."

"It will never happen."

Valentina's father had a reputation for a white-hot temper, but he was in such a hurry to leave, he disappeared without slamming the door behind him. It would be no surprise to Vincenzo if word of his forthcoming marriage to Valentina made the evening news. By tomorrow anything could happen. He sent a text to the woman he adored.

Francesca was in the middle of an operation when she heard the ding on her phone. Half an hour later she read his text.

Bellissima? Stefano just left my office. He's on the warpath. Warn your father. I'll meet you at your apartment after work. We'll take Artur

and drive to the palace to talk to my mother.
I have the best news that will change everything for her and us.

Francesca jumped for joy and texted him
back.

I'll let Dad know about the visit and be home
by five fifteen waiting for you.

Vincenzo arrived five minutes after she got
home. The second she opened the door, he
swept her in his arms. Artur's barking went
ignored while they kissed as if it were their
last. She pressed her forehead against his.
"Your news made it impossible for me to get
any more work done today. I thought I would
die until I was in your arms like this."

"When I got your text, I wanted to drive
straight to your office," he cried, covering her
with kisses, unable to stop.

"I love you so much, Vincenzo. You have
no idea. We'd better go inside before everyone sees us."

"Do we really care?" One more kiss before
he let her go so they could be private. She
settled the dog. "Now tell me everything that

happened with Valentina," she begged as he pulled her down on the couch.

"When I told her we both knew it wasn't my child, she admitted it, but she refused to get a DNA test and insists we marry. At that point I realized Stefano is driving all this. I knew there was nothing else to talk about and left. Later in the day he burst in my office."

She kissed his chin. "Valentina's father is scary. He just charged in?"

"That's his way. He said an announcement of my wedding plans to Valentina will be in the news by morning. I warned him not to do it because I wasn't the father of Valentina's child. He called me a liar. I told him to call your father for the facts. In his rage, he charged right out again."

She straightened and gazed into his incredibly blue eyes. "I doubt he's ever been challenged like this in his whole life. Poor Valentina."

"She's terrified, but after Stefano confronts your father, things will change."

"Maybe. Years ago, Dad told me Stefano was more impossible than their father and that's saying a lot."

"Let's not worry about it right now. We

need to leave for the palace. I told my mother to expect us this evening. When I tell her that Valentina lied to her, it will turn things around. She'll realize I've been speaking the truth all along. It won't be long before she's crazy about you and Artur."

He started kissing her. Like déjà vu her phone rang, interrupting them. The ringing stopped, then began again. "I'd better let you get it." He stood up and helped her to her feet.

She reached for the phone on the counter. Her eyes flew to his. "It's my father." Francesca put her phone on Speaker so he could hear their conversation and greeted him. "I take it you heard from Stefano."

"After talking to my brother, it's clear he's not about to let this go and has already gone to the newspapers to spread another lie. We both know he wants to get his hands on Vincenzo's timber assets. It's clear he doesn't care whose baby it is as long as Vincenzo's mother is convinced it's his. I fear it will be a fight to the finish. I'm afraid this is up to the two of you, Francie. Be assured your mother and I will back you in anything."

"You're wonderful! But Dad—I don't want you hurt."

"Our good friends will always be our good friends no matter what happens. Need I say more?"

Francesca had broken out in tears. "I don't deserve you."

"Nonsense. If I have a concern, it's for Vincenzo's mother. Does she know the truth?"

She glanced at Vincenzo. "Yes, but she doesn't believe it yet. He and I are visiting her in a little while and will explain everything. We're committed. Vincenzo isn't anxious, Dad."

"Then all should be well in the end. Let us know what we can do to help."

"You already have. I'll call you later."

She hung up and whirled around. "What are we going to do?"

"I'm not worried."

"My concern is your mother."

He hugged her. "When she learns that Valentina told me the truth herself, she'll realize Valentina lied to her. Everything will be all right."

"I hope so. I'll take a quick shower and get dressed."

Francesca was glad she'd bought a new small-print sundress with a jacket the other day. The aqua-and-blue flowers on white had caught her eye. On impulse she bought a pair of heeled sandals in aqua.

"While you do that, I'll get Artur ready to go with us and bring his crate."

"Mamma will love him."

She smiled to herself. Maybe her dog would be the miraculous clay that won over Vincenzo's mother.

"We'll stop for some pasta in Scuol before we reach the palace."

"Perfect."

Francesca hurried to her bedroom. Once she was dressed, she brushed out her freshly shampooed hair and put on some mascara and frosted coral lipstick. As a final touch, she replaced the gold stud earrings with aqua-colored starbursts. Now she was ready to go.

When she entered the living room, Vincenzo took one look at her and let out a whistle that sent the dog scrambling around. "Sorry, Artur. Your mistress is so dazzling, I forgot where I was and what I was doing."

"Thank you. Though I don't believe a word of it, you're very good for my ego."

His eyes danced. "Remember the board meeting? The men were so smitten, they

would have kept you there half the night if I
hadn't been around to claim you."

"Do you hear all this nonsense, Artur?"
She reached down to pick him up. "Come on.
You're coming to the royal palace with us and
need to be on your best behavior, especially
around Vincenzo's mother. She's the one we
have to win over. Mothers are important. I
love mine. Vincenzo loves his. The trick is
for her to love all three of us."

CHAPTER TEN

A FEELING OF RELIEF washed over Vincenzo when they reached the palace. For the first time as an adult male, he knew joy. The woman he loved heart and soul clung to his arm as they climbed the stairs to the second floor. The palace guards stared in wonder.

Using his other hand, he carried the crate with Artur inside it, loving this experience like no other. His euphoria was so deep, he didn't realize Bella was already hurrying toward them.

"You have to be the famous Dr. Linard."

Francesca smiled. "You're Bella who along with your brother used to catch fish in the stream with nets."

His sister chuckled. "We had to be resourceful so no one knew what we were up to." She knelt down to look at the dog. "Artur!

You're adorable." She looked up at Francesca. "He reminds me so much of Karl, it hurts." She got to her feet. "I'm so happy to meet you."

"I've been excited to meet Vincenzo's young partner in crime."

"Hey, you two," Vincenzo muttered. "*I'm* here too."

Both women burst into laughter. It thrilled him they were already acting like friends with secrets.

"I've been in Chur all day doing a fund-raiser and just flew back. Mother has been trying to reach me and asked me to come to the drawing room. I didn't know you would be here, brother dear. This is exciting."

"Let's hope it stays that way. I told Mother that Francesca and I were coming to talk to her again."

"I see." She patted Francesca's arm. "No matter what, you two have my vote." He could always count on her.

"Let's go in and we'll get the dog settled."

Bella opened the doors and the three of them entered the drawing room. No one was there yet. He put the crate by the love seat and reached inside. Francesca took the dog from him and put Artur on her lap. Bella knelt down in front of her to play with him. He wiggled and licked her.

As they were laughing at his antics, their mother came in with a large brown envelope in her hand. Vincenzo got up from the love seat and walked over to give her a hug.

"I see you've brought her and her dog."

Her unhappy mood hadn't changed. "He looks so much like Karl, we thought you'd like to meet him."

"I don't appreciate it, not when we have very serious things to talk about." She walked over to her favorite chair near the love seat and sat down. Then his grandparents came in the room. He got up to help his grandmother before pushing his grandfather's wheelchair over by the couch.

Vincenzo smiled at Francesca. "I'm glad we're all here because I have important news that is going to change all our lives. The other day I flew to Milano and met with Valentina. I learned from her own lips that she's pregnant with another man's child."

"That's not true!" his mother cried out.

"I'm afraid it is, Mamma."

"But that's impossible. Stefano—"

"Stefano refuses to face the truth," Vincenzo broke in. "What he needs to do is help Valentina deal with her life. Surely my own family knows me well enough that if the baby were mine, I would have insisted on marrying Valentina immediately."

"We know that!" Bella jumped up to hug him. "You're the most honest, decent person I've ever known in my life and I couldn't be happier for you and Francesca."

Her words meant the world to Vincenzo who gave her a big hug.

"Then what's this?" his mother blurted. "It was delivered to me a short time ago." She opened the envelope and took out the front page of Milano's *Corriere della Sera*. Stefano had done the deed, all right.

Francesca exchanged glances with him as his mother read the headlines. *"Bells from the Duomo di Milano will ring out on September eighteenth for the wedding of Princess Valentina Visconti to Prince Vincenzo Baldasseri..."*

Bella looked concerned and sat down next to Francesca and the dog. She had a heart of gold.

"Stefano had that printed to put pressure

on me and Valentina, but it won't work. He's been like a runaway train that couldn't be stopped."

His mother looked stricken. "Valentina wouldn't have lied to me, Vincenzo. She's a decent, wonderful girl."

"I agree—however, she didn't have any choice. Stefano has a stranglehold on her. He came to my office this afternoon to intimidate me with this fake headline announcement. He threatened me with a lawsuit for breach of contract to marry."

"Lawsuit?"

"Yes, Mamma. I told him it was the other way around. She broke *our* engagement. That's when he said it was because I'd neglected her. I told him that was an untrue statement because my visits to the palace were recorded by my pilot and I never missed one. I could submit them and photos in evidence to the court."

His mother put a hand to her throat. "I—I don't believe what I'm hearing."

"That's because you're a good woman, Mamma. But he has a history of having done bad things, especially to Francesca's father. He's hoping the Visconti family can finally lay claim to our timber business by my marrying Valentina. He's out of control. It's tragic that he can't love his daughter and help her during her pregnancy."

"I just can't comprehend this." She'd gone a little pale. "Your wedding has been planned. Every detail. Valentina loves our family and wants to be a part of us. We love her. She's the perfect princess. This simply couldn't be happening. I've wanted her to be my daughter-in-law. Marcello and I talked about it a year ago."

"I know, but those were your dreams, not mine or Valentina's. She's having another man's child which means she's in love with someone else. Not me."

Tears continued to pour down his mother's cheeks.

"I'm sorry you're so distressed. Why don't I walk you to your room so you can lie down?"

"No. No—"

"Bella? Mother probably needs a doctor. Would you find Elsa?" His grandfather's caregiver could take her vital signs.

"I'm on my way. She'll know what to do."

Suddenly Francesca got to her feet holding the dog, and approached his mother. "Princess Baldasseri? I'm so sorry you're in this much pain and I'm going to leave. You've received a terrible shock and both of you need to talk things out." She looked at Vincenzo. "Maybe one of your security men could drive me home? Please?" The pleading in those compassionate brown eyes left him with no alternative.

This had to be Francesca's finest moment. He thought he'd loved her before tonight. But this sacrifice on her part sealed her to him forever.

Just then Elsa came hurrying in the drawing room with a stethoscope around her neck. Bella ran over to Vincenzo while Elsa checked out their mother. She checked her vital signs and gave a nod that she was all right.

Relieved by that news, he put a hand on his sister's arm. "Francesca wants to go home," he whispered.

"Can't say I blame her."

No. Tonight had turned into a disaster. "Would you walk her outside the palace and ask one of the security men to drive her back to Zernez?"

"Of course. *I'd* take her, but I'd better not leave Mother."

"Agreed."

Vincenzo kissed her cheek, then walked over to Francesca. "Bella will see you out. I'll phone you in a little while. I love you so much." He kissed the side of her neck before picking up the dog and opening the crate door. "In you go, Artur."

"Thank you." Francesca avoided his eyes as she carried it out of the room with Bella at her side. Vincenzo followed them.

When he'd said he would endure anything to be with Francesca, he'd meant it. But they were already paying a high price for their happiness at the expense of his mother's health. He pulled her to him one more time.

"I know you're blaming yourself," she whispered against his neck. "But we made our decision together and we'll get through this."

"With you holding on to me, we already are." He pressed a kiss to her temple. As the women went down the staircase, he returned to the drawing room.

His mother was wiping her eyes. "I'm sorry, Vincenzo."

"So am I," his voice grated. The love of his life had put his mother's needs ahead of everything else. What an angelic woman.

"I hadn't intended to cause all this trouble, *mi figlio*."

"I know you didn't. It's going to take time for you to get over your disappointment about Valentina. Do you think you're ready for bed? We can talk in your room."

"I do think I need to lie down. We'll talk tomorrow." He helped her up. "Good night," she murmured to his grandparents who'd sat there the whole time without a word.

"Don't go away," he said to them in an aside. It was time he got to the bottom of their strange behavior. What was going on in their minds?

The housekeeper was there to help their mother get ready for bed. He kissed her good-night and went back to the drawing room only to discover that his grandmother had left the room.

"Nonno? Why didn't Nonna stay?"

"She wasn't feeling well. I rang for Elsa to take her to our room and examine her. From there she was taken to the hospital in an ambulance."

"What?"

"Thank heaven you came back so I could

tell you," the older man called out. "It's her heart."

"What do you mean her heart?"

"She's had a heart condition for about a year." His grandfather had been weeping. It brought tears to Vincenzo's eyes.

"Why didn't you tell me a long time ago? I don't understand."

"Because you had enough on your plate with your father's death and the arranged engagement to Valentina. With the added burden of taking on Rini's duties, she felt you'd suffered enough and didn't need to know her health problems. She swore everyone to secrecy, especially the doctor and Elsa."

"Poor Nonna. I wish I had realized so I could have done more for her."

"No, no."

"Please don't keep anything more from me, Nonno. I need the whole truth. How is she really?"

"The doctor will let us know if this episode is serious. So far she has recovered from various incidences and most likely she'll recover from this one without problem. Thanks to Elsa—she got her to the hospital fast. My son—" He pulled on Vincenzo's arm. "We have another secret, but she insists on being the one to tell you."

"What do you mean?"

"We've kept it for a long time, but now it's necessary that you know all about it. As soon as the doctor says you can visit, she'll be waiting to unburden herself to you. I urged her to tell you much sooner, but she was hoping for a different outcome."

Another outcome? Vincenzo couldn't imagine. "About what?"

"About you and Valentina."

"Why didn't you tell me?"

"Because I didn't know about this secret until after I discovered what your *nonna* had been doing. She swore me to secrecy. I love her and told her I wouldn't say anything, but after tonight, I know she's ready to tell all."

Vincenzo couldn't imagine. "I'm leaving for the hospital now and will stay all night if I have to. Bella will stay with Mamma. Will you be all right?"

"Of course. I have Elsa."

"Francesca and I will be back."

"You really love that girl, don't you?"

"With all my heart and soul."

"I know how that feels." He patted Vincenzo's arm.

"Take care, Nonno. See you later."

Vincenzo rushed out of the palace and drove to the hospital. He knew the way to the area reserved for their family on the top floor. A cluster of staff nodded to him. The attending physician walked over. "Your grandmother had a little upset, but is responding well to treatment and will be able to go home tomorrow."

"That's wonderful. Can I go in and talk to her?"

"Of course. She'll love seeing you."

Relieved to hear the good news, Vincenzo entered her private room and walked over to the hospital bed. "Nonna?"

"Vincenzo—I'm so glad you're here."

"Thank heaven you're going to be all right."

"I am now that you've come. It pains me that after you brought Francesca to the palace so we could get to know her, chaos ensued because of Stefano. Now you've had to drive here because of my emergency, but I'm fine."

"The doctor said as much. Nonno told me about your bad heart. You never breathed a word of it."

"Because I've never wanted to be a fuss to anyone."

"You're a saint."

"Hardly." She chuckled. "Think about it. Your mother has suffered so much from losing your father, I didn't want to add to her anxiety. She's missed him so terribly, I believe that's why she has counted on you and Valentina to fill part of that void. Hopefully tonight's revelations have opened her eyes a little, but it will take time."

"No one knows that more than I do. But now I want to know about the secret you're hiding with Nonno. What's going on?" He pulled a chair over to the bed and sat down.

"You're going to be shocked."

Vincenzo took a deep breath. "I'm listening."

"What I'm about to tell you could end up in a tragedy."

"For whom?"

"Valentina and you."

"What?"

"Just hear me out. That girl is in the most serious trouble of her life and has been confiding in me ever since your engagement."

He was incredulous. "You've been her friend all this time?"

"Yes. She couldn't go to her mother who's terrified of Stefano. So is Valentina. Absolutely terrified. The bottom line is this—she's been in love with one of the security guards at the palace for a year and a half, named Alessandro Piero. When Stefano caught them together in the garden kissing one day, he was dismissed on the spot and served a six months' jail sentence."

"You're kidding!"

"He's made it impossible for Alessandro to get a decent job and has treated her abominably."

Vincenzo shook his head. "I know from Francesca's father that Stefano was always difficult, but to imprison a young man and ruin his life…"

"It's irrational. The next day Stefano phoned your parents to arrange the engagement and plan your first meeting. He chose the right moment to get in touch with them. Since your father and mother felt it was time for you to choose a bride, they were amenable to the idea. After I met Valentina, I could see how lovely and charming she was. I encouraged her to come for visits.

"Most of the time you weren't here. Before long I realized neither of you were in love, but both of you were prepared to do your duty. In time she lowered her guard and told me the truth about her wretched life. When Alessandro was released, Valentina sneaked out of the palace to see him. He was staying with a friend. Of course, he knew she was engaged to you, but he knew why. They managed to meet in secret and then she became pregnant."

"So *that's* why the engagement was broken." It was all making so much sense.

"Yes. Valentina couldn't marry you when she was in love with Alessandro and carrying his baby. She went to Stefano with the excuse that you had lost interest in her and that's the reason why she didn't want to be engaged. Secretly she and Alessandro planned to run away and get married. Stefano became enraged and insisted that she do whatever was necessary to win you around."

He got to his feet. "By then I was totally involved with Francesca whom I adore."

"Anyone can see that." She smiled. "So Stefano went to the media to create a scandal. According to Valentina he wanted to force both of you into court. When she found that out, she ran away before her father could find her and called your grandfather who told me what happened.

"I—" her voice faltered, "I told Elsa to hide and protect her until you were told the truth. One of the maids is Elsa's relative and she's been bringing her food. I'm afraid your mother is going to be shocked when she learns what we've done."

He smiled. "You and Nonno, plotting together."

"Yes, he's used to my ways. We've done it for years."

"Well, don't worry. Mother won't know a thing because I'll get Valentina out of the palace to a safe place. Stefano would never dream you've been helping his daughter and he'll never think to look for her here. Please get better and come home soon."

"I knew we could count on you."

"As I have counted on you all these years. We're in this together."

"We knew you'd fix this when you heard the truth. That's because you're honorable like your grandfather and I know you care for Valentina."

"I do, and I want to help. Nonna? There's

no one in the entire universe kinder than you. But you've done enough and need to rest so your heart can heal. I'll take care of everything once I get back to the palace."

"But what about Francesca? That poor dear girl. She saw your mother's suffering. The look on her face when she told you she wanted to leave the palace—I'll never forget the love I saw in her eyes for you. How sad for this to happen when you've fallen in love… She must be beside herself."

"She and I are solid like you and Nonno. When she hears this story, she'll do anything to help. Valentina is her blood cousin. Remember that Francesca's own father was in the same situation with Stefano before he and her mother left Milano. Francesca is a saint as you're going to find out. One day soon I'll tell you all the wonderful things about her."

"Tonight I found out how unselfish she is. I can't wait to get to know her! Unfortunately it might take a little more time for your mother to remove the blinders and be convinced."

"It's going to happen, Nonna. I love you, and I'll see you at the palace tomorrow."

He kissed her cheek and dashed out of the hospital. With his head spinning, he rushed to the car. Forget phoning Francesca. He needed to see her, even if it meant she had to call in sick at work tomorrow. He sent her a text to say that he'd be at her apartment in twenty minutes.

Francesca had gone to bed in tears. After she read Vincenzo's text, she could breathe again and put on a robe over her nightgown. When she opened the door, their gazes met for a heart-stopping moment before he crushed her in his arms. "I can't believe our evening ended the way it did, Francesca."

"I know." She moaned. "I love you so much I've been in agony. But seeing your mother's unhappiness made me realize it's not going to work."

"Oh, yes, it is," Vincenzo murmured before kissing her nonstop. "I couldn't get to your apartment fast enough to tell you what I've learned since you left. Come and sit with me." He reached for her hand and pulled her down on the couch with him. "Where's Artur?"

"In my bedroom asleep in his crate."

"For once that's good. After you left, I took my mother to her room. She needed to go to bed. When I returned to the drawing room I found my grandfather alone. When I asked about my grandmother, he said she hadn't been feeling well. Elsa sent for an ambulance to take her to the hospital."

"Oh, no—that means our relationship must have upset her too."

"No, my love. Listen to me. Nonno explained she has a heart condition, but has kept it quiet for the last year."

"Are you serious?"

"Afraid so. Tonight it acted up, but when I went over to the hospital, the doctor said the treatment was working and she'll come home tomorrow."

"You've been to see her already?"

"Yes, and I found out she's keeping another secret as well." He smiled. "This one will astound you."

She studied him. "You sound different. Happy. What's this news I'm not going to believe?"

"You'll have to be patient. This story goes back to the first part of July a year ago when my parents announced the news I'd been dreading all my adult life."

"I'm afraid I know what's coming."

"You guessed it, but just stay with me for a few minutes. It's important."

This was a new Vincenzo. She smiled. "Go on. I'm dying of curiosity."

He kissed her features. "I'd just come in from a day of hiking with Luca and some females we'd met."

"Females, huh."

He grinned. "My father called me into the study. Out of the blue he said it was time for me to settle down. My spirits plunged to new depths. He announced that he and Mother had finally found the right woman for me and wanted us to meet officially."

Francesca swallowed hard. "You mean Valentina."

"Exactly. Her parents had approached mine. They said they could search the world over and not find a better husband for their daughter than Prince Vincenzo of the House of Baldasseri. According to her mother, Princess Valentina spoke more highly of me than any other eligible prince in Europe and wanted to meet me. I couldn't imagine what had prompted Valentina to say those things."

"You're not a woman, Vincenzo. I fantasized about you over those videos before I ever met you in person," came her honest confession.

"Francesca..."

"It's true. Keep talking."

"I concluded that her family had picked my family for underlying financial reasons."

A groan came out of Francesca. "That I can also believe."

"So our first meeting was arranged by both sets of parents, but it was through my grandmother I've found out why. Within a few days of their phone call, we attended a regatta held on Lake Garda where we joined with the Visconti family.

"I already knew what Valentina looked like. She was attractive and we got along well enough. Though she acted like she was happy, I knew it couldn't be true. But like me, she was trying to honor her parents, so I gave her the benefit of the doubt. A few days later we went through the formal engagement that sealed our fate."

Francesca's heart thudded painfully during the silence that followed. "And?"

"This is where the tale gets interesting. Once engaged, Valentina came to the palace to get to know my family. I knew mother liked her, but last night when I talked to my grandmother, I found out Nonna and Valentina had developed an attachment they kept secret from everyone including my mother."

"Your grandmother?"

"Yes. It led to many future confidences. My grandfather knew all about it and kept quiet while he supported her completely."

"He's a wonderful man to be that loyal to his wife."

"Agreed. Over the last year Valentina came to the palace many times no one knew about, especially me. Nonna asked for Elsa's help to let Valentina in without my mother, Bella or myself knowing what was happening. Valentina told her parents she was visiting me, so she was never prevented from coming. My grandmother took her under her wing and they became the closest of friends."

"Friends?" Francesca cried. "And you knew nothing about it?"

"Not a clue, but what Nonna told me a little while ago has rearranged my entire universe."

"Darling—" Francesca felt she would burst if he didn't explain. "Please don't keep me in suspense any longer."

"All right. The bottom line is, Valentina

has been in love with one of the guards at the Visconti Palace for a year and a half."

"You're kidding!" As Vincenzo continued to explain, Francesca couldn't believe what she was hearing.

"When Stefano saw them kissing in the garden, that's when he contacted my parents to force a meeting and engagement. Not only that—he fired the guard and put him in jail for six months. He froze his bank account too."

She cringed and clung to him. "What a ghastly man. When I think how he treated my father... It's horrifying that a royal like Stefano believes he can destroy people's lives that way with enough money and power."

"Nonna said Valentina and her mother have lived in fear of him for years. Now we know why. Valentina had to make up the lie about my being uninterested in her so she could break our engagement. To her shock, Stefano forced her into trying to get engaged again by threatening to go to the media with a scandal she'd never live down."

"Oh, Vincenzo. More than ever, I understand what my own father had to go through to escape his brother. Now Valentina is going through the same terrifying experience."

"It's tragic all right. Once released from prison, Alessandro Piero had no hope of getting a decent job with his prison record. All doors are closed to him. He's been living with a friend. Valentina and he have been meeting in secret. Now she's pregnant with his child."

Their baby—

To think Francesca's cousin had fled to the Baldasseri Palace, fighting for her life. It was incredible.

Hearing Valentina's story had touched Francesca's heart. How terrible to be afraid of your own father. "I'm sick for her. Stefano has tried to ruin many lives. It has to stop. Those poor things." Her voice shook.

"I knew that would be your reaction, Francesca. Your tender heart is one of the reasons I love you so much. After I left Milano the other day, she ran away and came straight to the palace to see my grandmother. Valentina needs help. Elsa is hiding her in her own apartment until Nonna gets home from the hospital. She's safe for now. My grandfather is making sure of it."

"But this is so awful for her, Vincenzo. I

would help any woman in this kind of jeopardy, but she's my cousin who has been kept from our family because of Stefano. We have to do what we can for her. It's important to me."

"And *me*," Vincenzo emphasized. "She tried to do the decent thing and get out of our engagement the only way she knew how. I admire her for that more than I can tell you. It's criminal that she and Alessandro have nothing to fall back on. Stefano has seen to that and smeared all our names in his desire for revenge, but starting tonight the fight is on and he won't win."

"*Mio amore?* Let's drive Valentina to your chalet where she can be totally private and work things out with Alessandro."

"We could do that, but I have an even better idea. Do you think your parents would be willing to let Valentina stay with them for a short time? They're family and I wouldn't be at all surprised if your father hired Alessandro to work in his packaging business in Bern. For that matter I'd be happy to hire him to work for the timber company."

"I *know* they'd come to Valentina's rescue.

That's the kind of people they are, wonderful like you. I'm the luckiest woman alive."

"Now you know how I feel since meeting you."

A wave of heat poured through her.

"The point is, we know Stefano will cut off all money to her. Valentina and Alessandro will be destitute. But what no one knows is, when the engagement was broken, I held back some timber money our family would have given Stefano once we were married as part of the marital agreement.

"That money can now go to the two of them for a wedding present. I assured my grandmother it's all going to work out. Alessandro and Valentina can buy a villa anywhere they want and have enough to raise the child they're expecting. Stefano won't be able to touch either of them or their money."

Tears gushed from her eyes. "You're a man so much greater than other men, I'm speechless."

"Say that to me when we're old and maybe I'll half believe you."

"When are you going to tell your mother?"

"As soon as possible. When she sees Valentina with Alessandro, all will become clear and she'll learn to love you."

Francesca looked away. "Of course she'll understand everything, but that doesn't mean she'll want me to be with you."

"She will in time. Listen to me."

CHAPTER ELEVEN

VINCENZO HAD KNOWN Francesca would put up this kind of resistance, but he had news for her and would speak what was in his heart. He let go of her long enough to get down on one knee and grasped her left hand.

"I've been wanting to do this since the moment we met. I hope you realize your apartment is our home now. No more hypotheticals. Francesca Giordano Visconti? I'm asking you to marry me right this minute, and I won't take no for an answer." He pulled a gold ring with a solitaire diamond out of his shirt pocket and slid it on her ring finger.

"I never dreamed of being able to do what ordinary men do. I never had hope of loving the woman I would have to marry. When I took Karl into the clinic, I was in a very dark place for many reasons, unable to imagine happiness. To make matters worse, Daniel wasn't available to take care of my best friend.

"I looked up to see who had spoken and my eyes fell on you, Francesca, the most adorable female imaginable, shining like a star. You seemed to have come straight from heaven to delight poor earthly men like myself. My heart actually quaked."

She slid down and put her arms around his neck. "Mine leaped to see the Prince I'd fantasized over suddenly appear in front of me. It's leaping now. I want to be your wife more than anything in this world."

"Francesca—" He rolled her to him and kissed the daylights out of her. "Swear to me nothing will change for you."

"Nothing will, *il mio cuore*. Your mother has to be a wonderful woman to have raised a prince of a man like you. I believe it will all work out."

"When Nonna comes home tomorrow and tells Mamma everything she'll welcome you with open arms, Francesca."

"I pray that will happen. My parents already adore you. They're as crazy about you as I am."

"Why don't we call them and let them know our news."

"I bet when we tell them about Valentina and Alessandro, they'll come up with a solution. Being that she's their niece, I know they'll want to help. But first things first." She covered his handsome features with kisses. They were so engrossed, it took a long time before they came up for air and made the call.

The whole conversation was like music to Vincenzo's ears. By the time they'd talked everything through, it was decided he was marrying Francesca at the church of Saint Peter and Saint Paul in Bern. It was the church where her parents had been married. All they had to do was wait for his mother's blessing before they put their plans into action.

They hung up and Vincenzo pulled her into his arms. "I'm going to leave so you can get a little sleep before you have to be at the clinic in the morning." He kissed her once more. "I'll phone you with any news tomorrow. Stay safe and well for me. You're the most precious person in my existence."

A feeling of elation over the plans for their coming marriage filled his being so completely, he didn't remember the drive back to the palace. He sent a text for Fadri that he wouldn't be going into work. Instead, he would stay home with his family. He wanted to be there for all of them.

Just as Vincenzo expected, the morning news announced the imminent marriage of him and Valentina. Bella rolled her eyes and shut off the TV. By noon, his grandmother had come back from the hospital. The whole family sat around her in his grandparents' suite.

"You need to rest," his mother cautioned her.

"Stop worrying about me," she insisted. "I feel fine and there's something of vital importance Alfredo and I have to tell all of you. In a way it's a confession."

"Confession?" Vincenzo's mother frowned. He could tell she hadn't slept well.

She gripped her husband's hand. "It's about Valentina."

Vincenzo had never loved his *nonna* more than he did at this moment while she told her amazing story. His grandfather added more information. When they'd finished, his mother got up from the chair and clung to the backing. Tears streamed down her cheeks.

"Thank you for this. I wish Valentina had felt she could confide in me, but I understand her fear of Stefano. To think he gave that false news story to the media…" Her eyes fastened on Vincenzo. "My poor dear son. He not only abused his daughter to get hold of our family money, he abused you relentlessly. Can you ever forgive me for not believing you?"

He walked over and reached for her hands. "There's nothing to forgive, Mamma. I love you with all my heart, and we're going to help Valentina and the father of her baby. Do you know Francesca wanted to drive back to the palace last night and take her cousin to safety at the chalet?"

She shook her head. "Francesca sounds wonderful. I've been so heartless where your true feelings have been concerned."

"Only because of Valentina. I promise you're going to love Francesca just as much. I also have news on that score. Francesca's parents are going to let Valentina and Alessandro live with them and give him a job. I'm giving them the money I held back from Stefano." He smiled. "You're going to end up with three daughters to love as soon as you give Francesca and me your blessing so we can marry ASAP."

"Oh, Vincenzo—" She threw her arms around him. "You have it with all my heart. I know if Marcello were here, he'd be overjoyed too."

Bella's tear-filled eyes met his. So did the watery eyes of his grandparents. Miracles *did* happen.

He hugged his mother for a long time before letting her go. Now it was time to phone the love of his life with the glorious news. With another hug to his grandparents, he left their bedroom and hurried to his own suite to make the call.

"Francesca? How are things going at work?"

"I called in sick. Poor Daniel. Artur is keeping me busy, but it doesn't stop me from thinking about your mother and her affection for Valentina. Even when the truth comes out, that doesn't mean she'll be able to let go of her feelings."

"Guess what? My grandmother got home from the hospital this morning. While we were all gathered round her, she and Nonno told us their secret. My mother stood there with tears dripping down her face and begged my forgiveness for not believing me. She wants to love you. Everything has been settled, and she has given us her blessing."

Francesca's cry of joy was so startling, the dog started to bark. Laughing, Vincenzo held the cell away from his ear. "Amen, my darling. I'm leaving for your apartment right now and we'll phone your parents to make detailed plans. Let's plan the ceremony for next Saturday. I'll tell the family before I leave here."

"That's only three days away."

"It's not soon enough for me."

"I need to tell Daniel and make arrangements for kenneling Artur."

"There's a lot to do. We need the name of the bishop at the church in Bern. The ceremony needs to be arranged."

"What about a special dispensation?"

"It won't be a problem. I'll phone Rini. He and Luna will want to see us married."

"So will my brother and his girlfriend, Gina."

Two hours later their plans were made. Tomorrow morning they'd fly in the Baldasseri jet to Bern from Innsbruck and stay with Francesca's family. Her mom would take her shopping for a wedding dress.

Their marriage ceremony had been arranged for ten in the morning. After a reception at the Visconti villa, they'd fly back to Zernez and enjoy a two-day honeymoon. A longer one would come later.

They moved to the door. "As soon as I get back to the palace, I'll ask my friend Luca to be a witness."

"Call me tonight, no matter how late."

He cupped her face in his hands. "I promise. Take care of yourself, *tesoro mio*. I couldn't live without you now."

In three days' time he'd be Francesca's husband. They'd raise a family. Over time more Karls and Arturs would come along too. No man could be this happy.

Three days later

"Honey? Are you awake?"

Francesca sat up in bed. "I've been up for hours, too excited to sleep."

"I don't blame you. It *is* your wedding day."

"Oh, Mom, I love Vincenzo so much, I can't believe I'm going to be marrying my heart's desire."

Her mother swept in the room. "I can relate."

She got out of bed. "I know. Vincenzo makes me happy the way Dad makes you."

"All four of us are very, very lucky. Now come on. You need some breakfast and we've got to get you dressed so you're not late for your own nuptials."

"Never." Francesca grinned and hurried into the bathroom to start her day.

Rain had descended on Bern this amazing Wednesday morning of late August, but the inclement weather didn't bother Francesca. Nothing mattered because she was getting married to the man who'd haunted her dreams from that first day he'd brought Karl into the vet clinic. She wanted to look gorgeous for him and had bought a white Alençon lace and silk gown that both mothers and Bella said looked made for her.

The four of them had enjoyed each other immensely while out shopping. When morning came, they helped her get dressed. The lace hem of the graceful slender A-line gown swept the floor. Her mother placed an Alençon shoulder-length mantilla over her hair.

Vincenzo's mother gave her a Baldasseri family treasure which consisted of tiny pearls, diamonds and rubies. She fastened it around her neck and gave her a kiss on the cheek. "This belonged to my husband's mother." Francesca loved her already.

Holding umbrellas, her parents helped her into the limo waiting in the courtyard of the Visconti two-story Swiss villa. Through the rain they drove to the lovely church in the old part of Bern. Built in the mid-eighteen hundreds, it was renowned for its painted ceiling and windows.

Francesca's heart jumped around thinking about Vincenzo waiting for her as they escorted her inside the foyer of the edifice. They brushed her off as sounds of the organ and choir permeated the church. Her father reached for her left hand and pressed an object into the palm.

When she looked down, she saw it was a gold band with a blue diamond her dad had produced for her to give Vincenzo. He and her mother wanted Francesca to know how much they approved of her choice of husband.

Francesca felt overcome as she reached out to hug him. "No one ever had a better father than you, Papa. I love you." She put the ring on her least finger until the time came in the ceremony to exchange rings.

Her mother handed her a bouquet of white roses. "The next time we see each other, you'll be Vincenzo's wife. Nothing could make me happier."

"Oh, Mom—I love you both so much." They hugged before her mother slipped inside the doors. That left Francesca standing there with her father.

They looked at each other as the "Wedding March" started. He reached for her hand. With a smile he said, "I don't need to ask if you're ready."

No. She was practically floating with happiness. Since meeting Vincenzo she'd been an open book.

A church worker opened the doors into the nave filled to the brim with wedding guests and flowers near the altar. Her parents had made many friends over the years. Vincenzo's grandparents sat in front. To Francesca's joy, she saw Daniel and his wife! He beamed at her.

She and her father continued down the center aisle, but her eyes had centered on Vincenzo wearing formal ceremonial Baldasseri dress blue with gold braid. Her Prince was so handsome she would have fainted right there if her father weren't holding her up.

Next to him looking splendid stood the Crown Prince of San Vitano, Rinieri Baldasseri, Vincenzo's cousin. On his other side stood Francesca's darling brother, Rolf. He looked tall and princely in his own right. The last man standing up for him was his attractive childhood friend Luca.

The priest marrying them waited at the altar in ceremonial robes. On his other side stood Vincenzo's lovely mother in purple chiffon. Francesca's mother was gorgeous in lavender. Next to her stood stunning Bella gowned in light blue. At her side stood Princess Luna in pink. The magnificent sight would dazzle anyone, but it was Vincenzo who took Francesca's breath.

The priest smiled at them. "Dear friends and family of the bride and groom, we welcome and thank you for being part of this sacred occasion. We're gathered here to witness the marriage of Francesca Giordano Visconti and Prince Vincenzo Rodicchio Baldasseri. Every human has the desire to love and be loved. Today we celebrate their love.

"If the couple will clasp hands, please come before me while the others take their seats and we'll begin with a prayer."

Francesca's mother took the flowers from her and sat down with her father. Vincenzo's mother followed. Rini claimed Luna. Rolf and Luca sat on another pew. During that whole time, Vincenzo squeezed Francesca's hand, enthralling her.

The priest gave a beautiful prayer, then nodded to the two of them. "Francesca, Vincenzo? Have you come here to enter into marriage freely and with whole hearts?"

"Yes," they said at the same time.

"Are you prepared to love and honor each other for as long as you both shall live?"

"Yes," she declared.

"*And* after," Vincenzo added. It reminded her of their conversation in the meadow after Karl had died when she'd said Vincenzo would see his beloved dog again. It brought tears to her eyes.

"Are you prepared to receive children from God and raise them according to the law of Jesus Christ and His church?"

"Yes," they both responded firmly. Vincenzo gave her hand another squeeze she felt through her entire body. The priest eyed both of them.

"Because it's your intention to join each

other in Holy Matrimony, you will now declare your consent before God." He nodded to Vincenzo who said, "I, Vincenzo Baldasseri, take you, Francesca Visconti, to be my wife. I promise to stay true to you in good times and bad, through sickness and health. I'll love, honor and cherish you all the days of my life."

The priest turned to Francesca who made the same vow. She finished with, "I'll love and honor you through life and throughout all eternity."

Vincenzo flashed her a smile meant for her alone before they kissed without the priest having to say anything. She couldn't believe this was really happening. This magnificent man had just married her. Her joy was almost too much to contain. She didn't want their kiss to end.

"What God has joined together, let no man put asunder. I now pronounce you man and wife. You may exchange rings."

With trembling hands Francesca pulled the ring off her little finger and reached for Vincenzo's left hand. The blue of his eyes intensified as she slid the wedding band on his ring finger. The fire in those orbs rivaled the heart of the blue diamond.

She heard an unexpected intake of breath before he produced a wedding ring and put it on the ring finger of her left hand. Further examination showed it to be a Baldasseri family heirloom with a ruby and diamonds. "My great-grandmother's ring," he whispered as he slid his arm around her waist. "It matches the necklace around your neck. You're my wife, Francesca. No man can put us asunder now."

There was steel in his tone as glorious choral music accompanied by the organ filled the interior. It was a surreal moment for Francesca as they walked slowly down the aisle with Vincenzo's arm around her waist. Once they reached the foyer, they embraced their loved ones before walking out to the waiting limo.

Francesca saw news reporters taking pictures and videos. It wouldn't be long before people watching the news would wonder what was going on. Everyone would ask how Prince Vincenzo could be engaged to one Visconti woman, yet married to another within a matter of days.

But she couldn't worry about that right

now. Before Vincenzo helped her in the limo, he folded her in his arms. When he lowered his head to give her a husband's kiss, she was so on fire for him, she forgot everything else. That kiss would be splashed all over the news, but it didn't matter because she'd become Vincenzo's wife.

The rain had turned to drizzle. An indoor reception at the Visconti villa awaited them. Francesca's father stood at the table where she and Vincenzo sat with her mother, Rolf and Gina. Vincenzo's grandparents and mother sat with Prince Rinieri and Princess Luna. Valentina and her fiancé Alessandro had been put at another table also looking blissfully happy. All their friends had gathered round at other tables laden with flowers.

"Welcome everyone on this joyous day of days. There'll be time for all the toasts you want after we eat, but right now I want to make one to my new son-in-law. I've learned things about him that you don't know and never will. But they make me humbled and proud that he has become a member of our family." He raised his champagne glass to Vincenzo.

"Here's to the groom, a man better than

other men, who kept his head even while he lost his heart to my precious daughter. These two were meant for each other. To that I can attest and give my blessing. May your joy last through the eternities."

Francesca knew her father's heartfelt words had touched Vincenzo so deeply, he grasped her hand beneath the table and clung to it. She knew the tribute acted like a healing balm after what Stefano had put them all through.

The rest of the party passed in a kind of heavenly blur as they ate and laughed and enjoyed all the many tributes. Perhaps her favorite toast at the end of the reception came from Vincenzo's best friend Luca.

He got to his feet and raised a glass to him. "Dante once wrote that a great flame follows a little spark. Apparently there was more than a little spark the day Vince took his sick dog Karl to the vet. One look at the gorgeous Dr. Linard and he was lit by the brightest light in the firmament. May your happiness last forever."

Vincenzo squeezed her hand tighter.

"Thank you, Luca," she mouthed the words to him.

Francesca's mother smiled at her. "It's time

for you to change and get you to the airport for your honeymoon."

Honeymoon—

She shivered in excitement. Francesca had never gone to bed with a man. Now she was a married woman and couldn't wait to be loved by her husband who kissed her cheek. "Hurry," he whispered. "I'll be waiting for you in the foyer."

A thrill of desire darted through her as he helped her up from the table. She left the room with her mother and went upstairs to change into a new summer suit in spring green.

Her mom helped her out of her wedding dress. After they hugged she went down to the foyer where Vincenzo was waiting for her. Everyone had gathered round while she got ready to throw the bouquet.

She knew where she wanted it to land, but it accidentally ended up in Bella's hands rather than Gina's. Vincenzo's sister turned crimson.

He put his arm around Francesca's shoulders. Nuzzling her neck, he said, "I'm glad your aim was off. Gina has already found her happiness with your brother. Now it's Bella's turn. Shall we go, Signora Baldasseri? Our chariot is waiting."

It was late afternoon. There were more photographers outside the villa, but she ignored them. The limo drove them to the airport where they boarded the helicopter. They'd fly to the major airport in Innsbruck, then home. "It's been a perfect day," she murmured against his lips after they climbed inside.

"That's true, but it's only the beginning. I've arranged for my security staff to have my car waiting for us at the airport in Zernez."

"Am I horrible to be this impatient to get back to the apartment?"

"You mean *our* apartment, and yes. It thrills me that you're as horrible as I am to want to go to bed. I'm not sure I'll ever let you go again, so be warned."

Their flight lasted too long, but finally they landed and hurriedly got in his car and he drove them to the apartment.

He shut off the engine and turned to her. "As of this moment everything is under control and we are now on our honeymoon. Nothing or no one is going to interfere with what I've been looking forward to since the moment I laid eyes on my Christmas angel."

"What do you mean?"

"That's what you looked like to me. One of those adorable angels hanging on the Christmas tree full of light and sparkle and so damn beautiful I wanted to steal you away immediately. It took all my self-control not to kidnap you from the clinic and hide you where no one could find you but me."

"Vincenzo—" She laughed.

"It's the truth, my love. In case you haven't noticed, we're here, *mio amore*."

Her apartment was a sight for sore eyes. It was a glorious evening, warm and beautiful. "Stay in the car. I want to take everything inside first, then come back for you. I'll need your key."

Francesca handed it to him. He hurried up the stairs with the food they stopped for plus their bags. Her heart pounded wildly while she waited for his return. Little could she have guessed that when she'd picked this apartment on the internet in July, Prince Vincenzo would become her husband and race up the stairs into their new home. A fairy tale beyond fairy tales, one she'd cherish forever.

* * *

The interior felt like heaven to Vincenzo. He took the bags to her bedroom. *Their* bedroom now. After returning to the kitchen to put away the groceries in the fridge, he went back out, leaving the door open.

Francesca had gotten out of her car and lounged against it. Their gazes locked as he came closer and picked her up in his arms like the bride she was. Miraculously she fit there like she'd been made for him. Without effort he carried her slowly along the walk and up the stairs. His eyes studied every feature, still trying to believe this remarkable woman now bore his last name.

"You have no idea how long I've been waiting for you to carry me over the threshold. I'd harbored an irrational jealousy knowing the cousin I'd never met was your fiancée. It seemed cruel that I was being tempted like this when I knew you were as far from me as the planets and forbidden to me in every way. That's what made my longing for you harder to bear. That first night I cried my eyes out."

"Francesca…" He kissed her fervently. "I didn't know that. The beautiful Dr. Linard kept her secrets. The last thing I wanted to do was leave the clinic."

She traced the line of his mouth with her finger. "I never intended for you to know how attracted I was. You can't imagine my shock when you told me your engagement had been broken off. I was so happy I was giddy."

"You never let on, *squisita*!"

He closed the door with his foot and carried her through the apartment to the bedroom. Following her down on the bed, he began kissing her. This was different than all the other times they'd been together. They were man and wife and alone for the first time since the wedding.

"When I took those wedding vows, I promised to worship you with my body, and that's exactly what I'm going to do."

"I love you," she cried from her soul, "more than life itself!"

"Amore." He helped remove her suit, then took off his trousers and shirt. Before long they lay entwined on the bed, enraptured as they poured out their love for each other. To Vincenzo it seemed like after meeting Francesca, he'd been waiting years for this moment.

She was the personification of his every

dream, loving and giving. His desire had reached its zenith. For hours they were swept away by needs and longings that no longer had to be held back. Francesca had taken him to a place of pure enchantment.

At one point they both slept with his arm around her hips. When he awakened, he discovered her leaning over him while she smoothed some hair off his forehead. "Do you know you're the most beautiful man I ever saw in my life?"

"I'll take that as a compliment."

"I can't wait until we have children. Everyone will rave that they look like you."

"Our girls will inherit your beauty and I'll have to beat off the suitors."

She chuckled.

Vincenzo found certain places to kiss her that he knew drove her crazy with longing. "Do you want a baby right away?"

"The mention of Valentina's pregnancy has made me think hard about us. Are you anxious to start a family? Tell me the truth."

"I can't imagine anything more wonderful."

"Neither can I."

"I'm glad you said that because I'm afraid I didn't take precautions."

She gave him that fetching smile. "I noticed, and I'm ecstatic because I'm hoping we're pregnant right now. Artur needs competition so he won't get too spoiled."

Deep male laughter poured out of Vincenzo. "He's already hopeless in that department. So am I. Love me again, *mia moglie*." He rolled her gorgeous body against him. "I need you more than I need food right now."

"That tells me more than you know. Kiss me again, and again, and again."

EPILOGUE

*The Baldasseri Palace,
two and a half months later*

VINCENZO HELPED FRANCESCA out of his car. She clung to him.

"What's wrong, darling?"

"I was just remembering the first time you brought me to the palace so I could meet your mother."

He hugged her waist. "Since then a lot of water has passed under that bridge, and now we're *her* guests. Mamma has been dying to have a party. She's back to her old self which pleases me more than you will ever know. It's a good sign she's gotten past that grieving stage for my father. Our marriage has brought new joy to her life."

"You're right. The person I'm concerned

about now is Bella. She's marvelous, but I sense she's unhappy. You never talk about it."

"Heartache came to Bella's life in high school."

"I presume you're talking a boyfriend."

"Afraid so."

"Is it a secret?"

"It has been. When we get home tonight, I'll tell you what happened."

They walked past the guards and up the back stairway of the palace to the drawing room.

Francesca almost fainted at the room full of people. Gorgeous Bella sat with her mother on one of the love seats. The older woman got up immediately and walked toward Francesca, holding out her arms. "I'm so excited my newest daughter is here."

Vincenzo let go of her hand so she could run to her. "We're thrilled to be here, Princess Baldasseri."

"Call me Maria, please." Her tear-filled voice got to Francesca's heart. They hugged for a long time. "Can you forgive a foolish woman who refused to let go of her selfish dreams when we first met?"

Francesca stared into blue eyes so much like Vincenzo's. "There's nothing to forgive.

The son you brought into this world and raised is the love of my life. I'm so thankful you're his mother. No man can match him, and that has everything to do with you."

She patted Francesca's cheek. "I'm the one who's grateful my son had the wisdom to choose an angel from heaven to be his wife. That's what he calls you. I've learned a great deal about you over the last few months. Words can't express my sorrow that it took me so long to come to my senses. If Vincenzo's father were alive, he'd sing your praises. Welcome home. It's *your* home."

"Thank you so much, Maria."

"Francesca?"

She turned to see her parents over on another love seat. Her brother and Gina sat in chairs next to them. She ran over to hug them. "This really *is* a celebration."

Everyone was smiling. Near them sat Vincenzo's grandfather in his wheelchair with his wife at his side. She hurried over to kiss them. "You two look wonderful."

"So do *you*!"

That was the moment when she spotted Valentina and Alessandro who'd recently been married. Her cousin was a knockout and looked so happy. Why not? Her pregnancy was starting to show.

They hugged each other. "Valentina? Did you ever imagine the two of us meeting, let alone under these circumstances?"

"Never." Her blue eyes glistened with tears. "I can't believe what you and Vincenzo have done for us." She hugged her hard. "I love your parents so much, Francesca. Uncle Niccolo and Aunt Greta are saints, and my cousin Rolf is fabulous."

"I agree. He says the same thing about you. To think we're cousins, and it has taken this long. How are you feeling by now? I know you had a hard beginning with your pregnancy. I feel bad that you had to hide out here when you didn't feel well."

"Vincenzo's grandparents are angelic as you know. All of their family is. So are you and your family. Your goodness has turned my life and Alessandro's around. When I learned how kind you've been through all this, I wept because my father has kept us apart all these years. Having you in my life is like having a sibling. I can't thank you enough for all you've done for us."

"You went through a horrible time."

"So did you. My father was horrible to Vincenzo and ultimately to you."

"I'm just thankful that's all behind us and that you're happily married now."

"We are."

Alessandro broke in. "There are no words to express my gratitude for all you and your family have done for us. It's incredible."

Francesca gave a big hug to the handsome man who'd dared to love Valentina despite all odds. "I'm thrilled the two of you are together."

"We'll never be able to thank Prince Vincenzo enough for his wedding gift and all the help he has been."

Francesca took Alessandro aside. "Before we knew the truth of everything, I wonder if it was as hard for you to think of Valentina's engagement to Vincenzo as it was for me?"

He shook his dark blond head. "I don't want to even think about it now. Those were dark days."

"But neither of us ever lost hope, and now they're over."

"Yes. Valentina's mother is coming to live with us in Bern."

"She told me."

"Vincenzo is a miracle worker, Francesca.

248 FALLING FOR THE BALDASSERI PRINCE

Maybe your husband hasn't even told you yet, but his attorney Marko Fetzer is helping my mother with her divorce."

"Valentina said as much. Vincenzo says he never loses a case."

"That's wonderful to hear. Thanks to your husband, we now own a fantastic villa and are decorating a baby nursery. You'll have to come and stay with us."

"We'd love it," Vincenzo interjected.

While Francesca stood there loving every second of this, he slid his arm around her shoulders and pulled her close. "It's fantastic that everyone we love is here," he exclaimed, looking around. "We came with news, Mamma."

His mother got to her feet. "What is it?"

"In about six and a half months, you're going to be a grandmother."

"That means *we're* going to be great-grandparents!" Vincenzo's *nonna* proclaimed. "Happy day!"

Everyone else in the room got up and gathered round to congratulate them. She got hug after hug from her own family and Bella, then she turned to Valentina who smiled at her through tears. "Partners in crime."

They both laughed. "I want us to become

good friends, Valentina. When our children are born, I want them to get to know each other. It's taken way too long for you and me to get acquainted."

"We'll never let it happen again."

Vincenzo came up just then and put his arm around her waist. "We're due in the dining room for a celebratory feast." After such a difficult beginning, Francesca was incredulous this day had come. "Will you be able to eat?" he whispered in her ear.

"Yes."

"Thank heaven." He turned to Alessandro. "Speaking as the men in the family, morning sickness needs to be eradicated."

"You can say that again," Alessandro came back, "especially when she says she wants at least three children. She doesn't want ours to grow up alone."

"That I can understand."

Francesca laughed as they walked through to the dining room. Her brother came over and sat down on her other side. "Hey, sis. You look so happy, I think you're going to burst."

"You know you're right?" She kissed his cheek. "How are wedding plans going for you and Gina?"

"We're set for the twenty-first of December. That will give us the vacation to enjoy our honeymoon."

"Where are you going, or is that a secret?"

"A secret."

"So that means you're going to go to Chamonix. She'll love it."

"Don't tell Gina," he whispered. "She's never been there. Dad's renting a small chalet for us."

"Lucky you. If it weren't your honeymoon, Vincenzo and I would join you."

His brows lifted. "Have you two decided where to take a real honeymoon?"

"As someone once said—that train has left the station. We'll wait until our baby is born. Then we'll leave Artur and our child with the family and fly to somewhere exotic for a week."

"Only a week?"

"Any longer would be too hard on us and our children."

He chuckled. "Artur thinks he's your child."

"He *is* in his own way and has taken up residence in Vincenzo's heart."

"What about my heart?" Vincenzo poked his dark handsome head between them.

She looked up into his eyes. "It's as big as the great outdoors. Everyone here adores you and praises you for all you've done. It's disgusting how much I love you."

"Wait till I get you home and you can prove it to me."

Rolf burst into laughter as her face turned crimson. "Hey, Francesca? Do you want to hear something really funny?" he asked in a quiet voice.

"I'm not sure." She was still trying to recover from Vincenzo's private message.

"I heard your mother-in-law talking to Bella before you and Vincenzo got here. She had no idea I happened to be passing in the hall and had picked up on their conversation.

"Vincenzo's mother said, and I quote, 'After the engagement was broken, Vincenzo told me no more princesses for him. In his emphatic way, he claimed he was going to find the woman he wanted. Period! I think he's forgotten Francesca *is* a princess with a defunct title. I got my way after all!'"

"He got something much better, Mamma," Bella murmured. "A woman who will love him to the ends of the earth and beyond."

* * * * *

Look out for the next story in
The Baldasseri Royals trilogy
Coming soon!

And if you enjoyed this story
check out these other great reads from
Rebecca Winters

Reclaiming the Prince's Heart
Unmasking the Secret Prince
The Greek's Secret Heir

All available now!